A SHOT IN THE DARK

Longarm smelled something, and it wasn't the creosote bushes that grew nearby. Instead, it was the acrid tang of gun oil. A second after the scent drifted to his nose, he heard the unmistakable metallic sound of a cylinder revolving as somebody squeezed the trigger of a double-action revolver.

He threw himself into a roll. A bullet whined past him. As he rolled, he palmed out his Colt and lifted the gun as he came to a stop on his side. He'd seen the muzzle flash from the corner of his eye, so he had an idea where the gunman was. He triggered twice in that direction, then came up in a crouch and threw himself headlong behind a rock. A second bullet whipped past his head.

Longarm's nerves stretched taut. An eerie silence had descended over the darkness. He hated this sort of cat-and-mouse game, where the man who moved first was the one who died. At the same time, waiting could play right into the other man's hands and give him the opportunity to improve his position if he could do it quietly enough. The rattle of a rock moving sounded to Longarm's left. He pivoted in that direction, saw the looming figure, and fired. His bullets tore into the shape, which was little more than a patch of deeper darkness . . .

TABOR EVANS

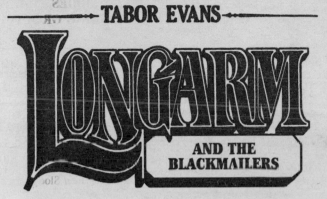

LONGARM

AND THE BLACKMAILERS

LONGARM AND THE BLACKMAILERS

A Jove Book / published by arrangement with the author

PRINTING HISTORY
Jove edition / October 2002

Copyright © 2002 by Penguin Putnam Inc.

Visit our website at
www.penguinputnam.com

ISBN: 0-515-13390-6

A JOVE BOOK®
Jove Books are published by The Berkley Publishing Group, a division of Penguin Putnam Inc., 375 Hudson Street, New York, New York 10014. JOVE and the "J" design are trademarks belonging to Penguin Putnam Inc.

PRINTED IN THE UNITED STATES OF AMERICA

10 9 8 7 6 5 4 3 2 1

Chapter 1

Naked, Longarm leaned back in the bed and clasped his hands behind his head. He let out a long sigh as the young woman leaned over his groin and took the head of his erect shaft into her mouth. Her soft lips locked warmly around the pole of male flesh. She had both hands wrapped around the lower part of Longarm's organ, and she stroked up and down with them, slowly.

Longarm closed his eyes and let the sensations wash over him. The gal was damned good at what she was doing. He could feel his climax building and knew that if she continued the French lesson for much longer, his seed was going to erupt in her mouth. Though he hated to think about her stopping, he said, "You might want to hold off there, otherwise you're going to get a mouthful."

She lifted her head and gave it a little toss to get the blond hair out of her eyes. "I don't mind," she said with a mischievous smile. "That way you can keep going longer once you actually get it in me. I intend to keep you at it all night, cowboy."

Longarm could only shrug and grin. Under the circumstances, whatever the woman wanted was pretty much all right with him.

She lowered her head and went back to it, using one hand now to cup his heavy balls and roll them back and forth in her palm. She was as naked as he was, and the way she was sitting beside him, her left breast was within his reach. He cupped the creamy globe and kneaded it for a moment, then began stroking the hard brown nipple with his thumb. That made her suck harder on his shaft. Longarm felt himself losing control and didn't even try to hold back any longer.

The woman took the first blast in her mouth, then lifted her head and aimed his organ so that the thick white seed spurted onto her face, painting her forehead and cheeks and chin with its hot slickness. She closed her eyes and moaned, and from the way her hips were jerking, Longarm knew that she had reached a climax of her own just from sucking him. She squeezed hard, milking the last few drops from his shaft so that she could lick them up. Then she rolled onto her back and lay there breathing heavily for a moment before reaching down to get a corner of the sheet and wipe her face.

"Sorry I sort of mussed you up," Longarm said, doing some heavy breathing of his own.

"Oh, no . . . I liked it." She reached up to her head and laughed. "There's even some in my hair!"

Longarm couldn't help but laugh, too. It had been a good long while since he'd run across a gal as lusty as this one.

Finding a beautiful blonde with an eastern accent in a little border trading post like Lajitas was odd enough. There was nothing around but thousands of square miles of empty, desolate West Texas desert and rugged, rock-strewn mountains. South of the Rio Grande, Mexico was pretty much the same. There was nothing here to have drawn a woman like Victoria Canfield.

Yet she was here, and from the first moment Longarm had stepped into the Lajitas Trading Post earlier tonight, he had known she was interested in him. Her eyes had followed him across the room to the bar, where he'd gotten a glass of warm beer and sipped it slowly to cut the dust of the long ride from the town of Alpine, north of here. Her bold stare intrigued him, and even though he was in the Big Bend region of Texas on business—lawman's business—he had given in to temptation and gone over to the table where she sat alone. She had accepted his offer of a drink and invited him to sit with her.

She wasn't a whore. Everything about her told Longarm that much. She was dressed in the same sort of low-cut blouse and colorful skirt as the Mexican women in the area, but the outfit looked even more exotic with her blond loveliness. She was well-educated but not stuffy and superior. Longarm liked her and was drawn to her right away. Clearly, Victoria returned the feeling.

So it came as no surprise to Longarm when they wound up in the small adobe hut where Victoria was living, a hundred yards from the trading post, both of them naked on the bed in a room lit by a single candle. And so far, Victoria was living up to everything her sensuousness had promised.

Longarm's organ had softened. Victoria cupped it in her hand and said, "How long before it'll be hard again?"

Longarm chuckled. "Well, I don't rightly know. I don't expect it'll be too long . . ."

She moved up on the bed, turned so that she was facing away from him, and swung a leg over his head and shoulders so that she was straddling him. When she lowered her hips and lay down across his chest and belly, her femaleness was only a couple of inches from Longarm's face. He felt her warm breath against his manhood.

"Why don't you lick me while we wait?" she suggested.

Longarm had to laugh again. Damn, she was the most brazen hussy he'd ever met!

But he wasn't going to deny her what she wanted. He brought his head forward, extended his tongue, and began running the tip of it along the fleshy pink folds of her femininity. She was wet already from her climax of a few

3

minutes earlier, and the juices began to flow even more as Longarm inserted his tongue into her core. While he was doing that, he used a finger to tease the crinkled brown bud between the cheeks of her rump. Victoria began panting, and her hands clenched on the solid muscles of Longarm's thighs. He felt his organ stiffening and rising into a new erection.

Nope, he thought, it wasn't going to be long at all before he was ready to go again. . . .

"That's the backside of hell. You know that, don't you, Billy?" Longarm had asked a week earlier as he sat in the chief marshal's office in Denver's federal building.

Billy Vail rustled the sheaf of papers in his hand. "I don't get to pick and choose where fugitives run off to," he said peevishly. "All I can do is send my deputies after them, wherever they go."

Longarm puffed on the thin black cheroot and blew the smoke toward the banjo clock on the wall of Vail's office. "I reckon you're right," he said, "but every time I go to West Texas, it's hot as blazes, and folks are shooting at me."

"Seems like you get shot at everywhere you go," Vail replied dryly. "You could get in a shoot-out in the middle of a church service, Custis."

As a matter of fact, Longarm reflected, he *had* gotten in a gun battle in church a time or two. But that was neither here nor there.

He leaned back in the red leather chair and cocked a booted right ankle on his left knee. "Who's the hombre I'm after this time?" he asked.

"The gent's name is Peter Braddock." Vail separated one of the papers from the stack in his hands and tossed it across the desk to Longarm. "He was an agent in the U.S. Customs Service, working out of the Laredo office."

Longarm looked at the document in his hand and observed, "Says here border smuggling's been awful bad around there lately."

4

Vail gave a snort of disgust. "Yes, and that was mostly Braddock's fault. He's been taking payoffs to look the other way for Lord knows how long. He probably collected a small fortune from those smuggling gangs below the border."

"Until one of the other agents found out about it," Longarm said, still scanning the report.

"That's right. And Braddock murdered him."

"Then took off for the tall and uncut?"

Vail nodded. "Braddock was raised in the Big Bend. His father had a ranch out there in the Chisos Mountains, back in the days when the Apaches were so bad."

"I hear-tell the Apaches still ain't given up on taking back that part of Texas."

"There's a band led by the war chief Alsate that's still hiding out in the mountains and raiding now and then. With the army and the Texas Rangers after them, though, they lay pretty low most of the time. You shouldn't have any trouble with them."

"Hope somebody's told that to ol' Alsate," Longarm said with a grin.

Vail ignored the comment. "Braddock's father lost the ranch and died a while back, and Braddock went to work for the Customs Service. I reckon he was probably crooked from the start. The main thing is, he's on the run now, and somebody's got to go in and get him."

"And that somebody is me."

"Don't go fishing for compliments, Custis. You know you're the best man I've got."

"Braddock knows the Big Bend like the back of his hand," Longarm said. "He won't be easy to find."

"I'm sure you'll manage. You can take the train part of the way, then there's a stage to Alpine. You'll have to rent a horse and ride on down into the Bend from there." A trace of wistfulness crept into Vail's voice as he went on, "Back when I was riding with the Rangers, I went on border patrols through there pretty often. I sort of miss it sometimes."

Longarm refrained from suggesting that if Vail missed the hellish place so much, he could go chasing after the murderous Peter Braddock his own self. Instead, he commented, "The Indians say that when the Great Spirit got through creating the world, He dumped all the rocks he had left over into the Big Bend."

Vail grunted. "They may have something there."

The trip had been long and hot and dusty, just as Longarm expected. His first stop was Lajitas. The trading post there was one of the few centers of activity in this desolate landscape. Farther up the Rio Grande was the settlement of Presidio. Longarm intended to go there next if he didn't turn up any leads to Peter Braddock in Lajitas.

What he had turned up instead was the stunning blonde named Victoria, and at the moment, he was digging his fingers into the firm round globes of her hindquarters and using his lips and tongue to bring her to yet another climax. When she stopped jerking and spasming and had caught her breath, she said, "I think you're ready now." She swung around to straddle his hips, facing him again.

Longarm's thick, meaty pole was as hard as a bar of iron. Victoria sank onto it, slowly filling herself with his maleness. About halfway down, she gasped, "Oh, my God! I don't know if I can take all of it! It feels even bigger going in me."

Longarm grasped her hips and surged up, sheathing another few inches inside her. Victoria gasped again. "Oh, yes! I want all of it!"

Longarm gave it to her, driving inexorably into her until his full length was buried in the core of her sex. The hot, velvety muscles inside her gripped him tautly. Slowly, both of them began to move, hips and pelvises thrusting against each other.

The pace gradually increased until their bodies were slamming together. The heat seething inside Longarm was looking desperately for a way out. Only one sort of release would satisfy that need. Longarm filled his hands with her breasts, squeezing and caressing, then urged her down on top of him so that he could put his arms around her. He continued thrusting hard into her as their open mouths met in a hot, urgent kiss. Victoria's tongue speared into Longarm's mouth. He met the invasion with a counterattack of his own, so that their tongues danced and circled wetly around each other. He slid his hands down the long, smooth line of her back and splayed his fingers on the cheeks of her rump. Holding her firmly in place, he drove as deeply inside her as he could and began to empty himself, his seed flowing out in spurt after white-hot spurt. Her own climax rolled through her at the same instant, causing her to flood his groin with her sticky nectar.

They held each other tightly as they spiraled down from the heights they had attained. Longarm's pulse was pounding as he came back to earth, and he could feel Victoria's heart thudding strongly against him. Both of them were covered with a thin layer of sweat despite the coolness of the nights in this high desert country.

As Longarm held her, the candle finally burned down and guttered out. Darkness enfolded them.

Without meaning to, Longarm dozed off. The short nap turned into a deep, dreamless slumber that lasted until morning. Longarm didn't wake up until sunlight lanced into the room through one of the windows.

He rolled onto his side and extended an arm, expecting to feel nude female flesh snuggled against him. Instead there was only the tangled sheet. Longarm raised himself on an elbow and opened his eyes. He shook his head to clear away some of the cobwebs that lingered from the deep sleep. He saw that he was alone in the room.

A second later, a soft footstep told him that someone was approaching. He darted a glance toward the butt of his Colt. The night before, he had coiled his shell belt and put it and the holstered revolver on a small table within easy reach of the bed. He didn't think anybody was about to ambush him, but he hadn't lived so long in a dangerous profession by taking chances. He reached over and wrapped his fingers around the polished walnut grips of the Colt.

"Oh, good, you're awake," Victoria said as she appeared in the doorway of the bedroom. If she noticed that Longarm was reaching for his gun, she gave no sign of it. "Come on. I want to show you something."

Longarm let go of the Colt, sat up, and swung his legs out of bed. As he stood up, he reached for his trousers.

"No, you won't need those," Victoria said. She stepped into the room and grabbed his hand, tugging on it impatiently. "Come on."

Longarm didn't know what the hell she was up to, but he didn't like the idea of going anywhere without either his gun or his pants, preferably both. Victoria wasn't going to be denied, though. She practically dragged him out of the room. Longarm was strong enough that he could have set his feet and stopped her, but he went along, curious as to what she wanted with him.

Victoria was dressed, not in the border peasant garb of the night before, but rather in boots, denim trousers, and a man's shirt with the sleeves rolled up. She led Longarm into the hut's only other room, which served as kitchen and dining room and parlor all wrapped into one. Still tugging on his hand, she steered him toward the door.

"Hold on," Longarm said. "You don't expect me to go outside buck naked, do you?"

"No one's going to see you," Victoria said breezily. "It's too early for that. Everyone at the trading post is still sleeping off all the beer and mescal from last night. Besides, we're just going around to the back. It won't take but a second."

Longarm still didn't like the idea, but his keenly honed instincts told him he wasn't facing any danger this morning, only potential embarrassment. He went outside with Victoria, his eyes narrowing against the brightness of the early morning sun. Despite the hour and the chill that lingered in the air from the night, the sun's rays felt hot as they fell against skin that was normally covered up.

8

He wasn't going to be happy if his backside got sunburned, Longarm thought.

"Around here," Victoria said. She circled the adobe hut, taking Longarm with her. When they got to the corner of the hut, he saw that a large, open, shedlike affair had been built behind it. He hadn't noticed that in the dark the night before. The thatched roof of the shed provided some shade but had enough gaps in it so that plenty of light came through.

Longarm stopped and frowned at the triangular arrangement of thin boards that supported a big piece of canvas that was tacked to more boards. That was an artist's easel, he realized, having seen such things a few times before in his life. On a bench at one side of the shed were a dozen or more small, earthenware pots, and as Longarm looked at them, he thought that they probably held different hues and shades of paint. He looked at Victoria and said in surprise, "You're one of those picture painters!"

"An artist, yes," she said, bobbing her head in agreement. "And I want to paint you, Custis."

Longarm frowned. "You mean . . ."

"That's right. I want to do a nude of you."

Well, if that didn't beat all, he thought. At least now he understood why Victoria had come to Lajitas and why she stayed here. She was an artist, and everybody knew that all artists were loco. One of them Longarm had read about was so crazy he'd cut off his own damned ear. Of course, that was better than some other things the hombre could've cut off, Longarm supposed.

"I don't know, Victoria . . ."

"Please, Custis? You're such a . . . a magnificent specimen of masculinity. I'd really like to paint you."

Longarm hesitated. He hadn't told her that he was a lawman or that he had come to this out-of-the-way part of Texas in search of a federal fugitive. He wanted to keep his real identity to himself as he poked around the border country looking for any trail that Braddock might have left behind. Since he couldn't really explain himself to

9

Victoria, he couldn't very well refuse her plea without risking offending her.

And being a gentleman, Longarm didn't want to offend a lady, especially one who had been so blasted cheerful about romping so lewdly with him.

"All right," he said. "It won't take too long, will it?"

Victoria smiled. "That depends on how well you can hold still."

Longarm bit back a muttered curse. "Where do you want me to stand?"

"Right over there," she said, pointing. "There, where the light is good."

Chastising himself as a damned fool under his breath, Longarm went across to the other side of the shed and stood where Victoria had indicated. "Like this?"

"Well, you can't just *stand* there. You have to strike some sort of pose. Turn a little and raise your arm . . ."

Feeling more foolish than ever, Longarm complied.

"That's better." Victoria pulled the bench with the pots of paint over by the canvas on the easel. She picked up a brush from the bench and dipped it into one of the pots. "Lift your arm a little more . . . move your right leg in front of your left . . . that's it . . . now throw your shoulders back and raise your chin slightly . . . My God, you look like some sort of noble Greek warrior, Custis! You could be on your way to Troy to rescue fair Helen. Perhaps I should call you Odysseus instead of Custis."

"Just don't call me late for supper," Longarm growled.

"Don't move now."

He couldn't see what she was daubing on the canvas. From time to time she leaned over to look around the easel and study him, and as he felt her eyes on him, an inevitable reaction began to set in. His face grew warm as his shaft slowly hardened, rising more and more toward a full erection.

Victoria giggled. "Custis, I'm afraid you're moving. At least part of you is."

"Blast it, woman," he said through clenched teeth,

"paint your damned picture and get it over with!"

She laughed again. "Great art can't be hurried. And I have to say, Custis, you are definitely a work of art."

Longarm closed his eyes. It could be worse, he supposed. At least in all likelihood, no one he knew would ever see the portrait that Victoria was painting.

And if they did . . . well, he'd just have to shoot them. That was all there was to it.

Chapter 2

Longarm never would have guessed what hard work it was posing for a picture. He was used to being still, though—being able to remain motionless had saved his life more than once when hostile Indians or owlhoots were looking for him—so he was able to maintain the pose until Victoria told him he could move again. Then he relaxed, rolled his shoulders to ease stiff muscles, and stretched his back. As he was doing that, he became aware that he was still naked. He had almost forgotten about that.

"As tempting as it is to take you back in there and ravish you," Victoria said with a smile, "I think I'd better fetch your clothes for you, Custis. Otherwise I'll never get back to the portrait."

"You ain't finished?"

"Oh, no. It'll take several sessions before the painting is complete."

Longarm frowned. He couldn't hang around here all day, or several days, no matter how pleasant the prospect might be. He had a job to do.

Besides, there was something vaguely disturbing about the idea of a grown man standing around naked as a jaybird while a gal painted his picture. Doing things like that might not have bothered those old Greek fellas Victoria had mentioned, but from what Longarm had heard about *them*, they'd got up to a lot of foolishness he didn't want any part of.

No, Victoria might not like it, but he was going to have to take his leave, Longarm decided.

While she went into the adobe to fetch his clothes, he wandered over to the rear wall of the building. Several canvases were leaning against it, stacked in front of each other. Paint dried mighty quickly in this hot, arid atmosphere, so Victoria wouldn't have to worry about the paintings getting smudged. Idly, Longarm started looking through them, pulling each canvas carefully away from the one behind it. The first couple of paintings were landscapes, and although he didn't know sic 'em about art, he thought they were pretty good. Victoria's brush strokes had captured the stark beauty of the desert and the mountains.

The next painting made Longarm frown a little. It was a portrait of a naked man. The fella was rather stocky but muscular, with blond hair and an intelligent face. Something about the eyes struck Longarm as being ruthless, but that might have been his imagination. Longarm didn't look too closely at the rest of the painting.

So he wasn't the first hombre to pose for Victoria back here, Longarm mused. The man in the painting probably had bedded Victoria before she painted his portrait, too. She'd made it plain that she was a woman with a strong appetite for the pleasures of the flesh. Longarm didn't feel any jealousy as the thought crossed his mind. He had long since passed the point where he expected every gal he met to have remained a blushing virgin until he came along.

Victoria came around the corner of the hut, carrying Longarm's clothes. Hurriedly, he put the paintings back the way he'd found them, but Victoria didn't seem to

13

mind that he'd been looking at them. She said, "Oh, you found the portrait I did of Peter."

Longarm frowned and said, "Peter?"

Victoria handed him his clothes. "That's right. You're not the jealous sort, are you, Custis?"

"Not a jealous bone in my body," Longarm told her honestly as he pulled on the bottom half of the long underwear.

He had a curious bone, though, and he was feeling a twinge in it right now. He remembered the description he had been given of Peter Braddock: stocky, dark blond hair, about thirty years old . . .

Just like the gent in the portrait.

"Well, good," Victoria went on, "because it didn't really mean anything. You're a much better subject than he was—and I mean that in every sense of the word."

Longarm buttoned his denim trousers and shrugged into his butternut shirt. "Does that fella live around here, or was he just passing through?"

"I believe he just stopped for a couple of nights in Lajitas. I'd never seen him before." Victoria shook her head. "I haven't seen him since then, either."

"He tell you the rest of his name?"

Another head shake. "Just Peter." She paused. "I don't know *your* last name, you know."

"It's Long, Custis Long." Longarm didn't see any harm in telling her that much.

Victoria glanced at the easel and murmured, "How very appropriate."

For the first time, Longarm looked at the painting she had started of him and saw that she had begun by sketching in some prominent anatomical features. He felt his face getting warm again.

"How long ago did this fella ride through?" he asked, getting back on the subject that was most important at the moment.

"Let me think . . . I know it was less than a week ago."

Longarm's pulse quickened. If the man in the painting

14

was really Peter Braddock, he was taking his time about retreating into the desert fastnesses of the Big Bend. He probably thought that no one would trail him here, or that if they did, he would be able to escape any pursuit because of his knowledge of the rugged country.

"This is Thursday, isn't it?" Victoria said. "Peter left here on Monday morning."

Three days, Longarm thought. Braddock was only three days ahead of him.

Then he reined in his excitement. He couldn't be sure that the man in the painting was Peter Braddock. But there was at least a chance the fugitive had been here in Lajitas only three days earlier, and Longarm couldn't afford to pass up such a potential lead.

"Did he say where he was going from here?"

Victoria frowned at him. "Why are you asking all these questions, Custis?" she demanded. "I thought you said you weren't jealous. Now you sound like you intend to go after Peter and . . . and thrash him or something!"

Or something was right. Arrest him, that was what Longarm intended to do. Or plug him, if Braddock put up a fight. *If* the hombre really was Braddock.

"I don't intend to thrash anybody," Longarm assured Victoria. "It's just that the gent in that painting looks like the man I came down here to Texas to do business with." There, that statement was true as far as it went.

"You don't know for sure?"

"I never met the man." Another honest reply. "All I know is what he's supposed to look like, and that his name is Peter Braddock."

Victoria looked a little less suspicious, but not much. "I suppose he could be the man you're looking for, then," she said slowly. "Is this . . . business of yours . . . something illegal, Custis?"

She thought he was a smuggler or a wide-looper or some other sort of owlhoot, Longarm realized. He said, "Not hardly. It's all legal and aboveboard, Victoria."

"You swear?"

15

"You got my word on that," he told her.

She relaxed even more. "All right. You seem trustworthy. I don't bring just any drifter or saddle tramp home with me, you know."

"Of course not."

"Peter mentioned that he was traveling on up the river. That's all I know."

"It's enough," Longarm said. "I'm mighty obliged to you." He started around the hut. "I got to get my hat and my gun."

"Wait!" Victoria called urgently. "You're not leaving, are you?"

He stopped and turned to face her. "I don't have any choice. I got to try to catch up to that gent while I still can."

"But . . . but I'm not finished with the painting!" Victoria gestured toward the canvas on the easel behind her.

"I'm sorry," Longarm told her, and meant it. "Maybe you can sort of put it aside, and if I can I'll ride back this way when my business is over, then you can finish it."

"But what if you don't ever come back?" She looked up at him, a mixture of anger and sadness on her lovely face. "Besides, there are so many things we haven't done yet."

She named a couple of them, and Longarm's mouth got dry and his pulse hammered in his head for a moment. Victoria was making it damned difficult to ride away from her.

In the end, though, Longarm knew what he had to do. He put his hands on her shoulders and bent down to kiss her, hard and fast and passionate. "If I can, I'll come back," he promised as he straightened. "Until then . . . well, they have a saying down here: *Vaya con Dios.*"

"*Vaya con Dios,*" she murmured.

Steeling himself, Longarm turned and went around the adobe hut. He got his hat and his gun as quickly as he could, then strode out of the hut and turned toward the

16

trading post. The night before, he had left his horse in the corral behind the squat adobe building.

He didn't look back as he walked away, but he couldn't help but wonder how those old Greeks had felt when they left their women behind and went off to war.

He got a breakfast of coffee, tortillas, beans, and chiles at the trading post, replenished his supplies, then asked the proprietor of the business about Peter Braddock, describing the fugitive as best he could.

The man nodded. "Yeah, I recollect a gent who looked like that passing through here a few days ago. He spent most of his time over at that artist gal's place." The man lifted his bushy eyebrows suggestively. "I figger you did the same thing, mister."

"That ain't any of your business," Longarm said, his voice cold.

The storekeeper lifted both hands and said quickly, "You're sure right, mister. None of my business a'tall."

"The fella I was asking you about, he rode upriver?"

"That's right. I sold him a little grub. He said he was runnin' low. But he didn't say nothing about where he was headed, if that's what you're fixin' to ask. And if there's trouble betwixt you and him, I don't want any part of it."

"No trouble," Longarm said, "just maybe some business."

"Like you said, it ain't none of mine."

The storekeeper was being cautious now, after he had told Longarm all that he knew. At least Longarm hoped he had learned everything there was to learn here in Lajitas. He picked up the bag of supplies he had bought and turned away from the trading post counter.

Five minutes later he had saddled up and was riding out of Lajitas. He still didn't look back, knowing that he would see Victoria's hut if he did so. He kept his gaze turned ahead, instead.

Longarm rode a rangy chestnut gelding that made him

look even taller than he really was, which was considerable. In high-topped boots, denim trousers, butternut shirt with a rawhide drawstring at the throat, and flat-crowned, snuff-brown Stetson, he could have passed for a range rider, a top hand who happened to be between jobs right now. The worn but well-cared-for Colt that he wore on his left hip in a cross-draw rig and the Winchester he carried in a saddle sheath were also the sort of weapons that a drifting cowboy might carry, but they gave Longarm an air of menace that said he might also be a shootist of some sort. His deputy marshal's badge and identification papers were tucked away safely in his saddlebags.

His lean face, dominated by strong features and a sweeping longhorn mustache, was tanned and weathered permanently to the color of old saddle leather. He had been in the West for so long—ever since the War ended—that he sometimes almost forgot that he'd been born and raised in West-by-God Virginia. He was a frontiersman now, and that was all he would ever be.

It was enough, Longarm thought.

Lajitas was not right on the river, but rather about a mile north of the Rio. On the other side was the Mexican village of Paso Lajitas, even tinier than the settlement built around the trading post. The road curved southwest from Lajitas until it reached the steep bluffs overlooking the border river, then followed the Rio Grande northwest toward Presidio, some fifty miles away. When Longarm glanced to his left as he rode along, he could see the deserts and mountains of northern Mexico. The craggy peaks looked close enough that he could reach out and touch them, though he knew they were actually several miles away. The mountains were known as the Sierra de Santa Elena, and the declivity through which the river flowed was called Santa Elena Canyon.

Longarm reined in when he reached the rimrock and looked both directions, up and down the river. Here in the Big Bend, the Rio Grande was not the wide, sluggish stream it was closer to the coast. Here it was narrow, and it flowed fast between the steep canyon walls. Splashes of white marked stretches of rapids. Longarm knew there were jagged rocks down there, their stony fangs waiting to tear the hulls out of any boats that came along, not that many did.

He hitched the chestnut into a walk. There were a few sheep farms and hardscrabble ranches between here and Presidio. He would stop at them as he came to them to ask about Peter Braddock. As long as Braddock stayed on this side of the river, Longarm was confident that he would track him down sooner or later.

Before midday, he had to hunt some shade. The sun's heat was too hot and brutal for both him and the horse. There was a good reason for the tradition of the siesta, Longarm knew, and he wasn't going to push his luck. He found a grove of stunted cedars and rode among them, then swung down from the saddle.

He hobbled the chestnut so that it could graze on the scanty grass without wandering off, then stretched out on the ground underneath a cedar, leaned back against the trunk, and tipped his hat down over his eyes. A few minutes later he was snoring softly.

Longarm woke up in the late afternoon and rode on upriver for several more miles. The lowering sun was still hot, but it was bearable now. He came to a farm and asked the peon who was working in the rocky field if another man had ridden along here in recent days. In the mixture of Spanish and English that was spoken here along the border, Longarm described Peter Braddock.

The Mexican nodded and waved a hand upriver. "*Si,* this man he rides by, but he does not stop."

"In a hurry, was he?"

"No, senor. He takes the time, like he has no cares in the world."

Longarm ran a thumbnail along the line of his jaw and then tugged on his right earlobe as he thought. For a renegade Customs agent who had taken bribes and then mur-

19

dered a fellow agent, Braddock was sure taking a mighty leisurely approach to flight.

Of course, maybe the man he was following wasn't even Braddock, Longarm reminded himself. In that case, he was wasting his time.

Still, Longarm had never been one to believe overmuch in coincidence. The gent called himself Peter and matched Braddock's description. That was enough to keep Longarm on his trail, at least for a while longer.

"Muchas gracias," he told the farmer, then rode on. The man waved as Longarm rode away.

That night, Longarm camped in another cedar grove. The next morning, he came up on a flock of sheep and asked the boy who was herding the woollies about Braddock. The youngster had seen such a man riding slowly upriver. Longarm tossed the boy a coin in appreciation, bringing a big smile to his face.

Ever since leaving Lajitas, Longarm had been pushing the chestnut at a pretty good pace. Now he urged the horse into an even faster trot. He was cutting the gap between him and the man he was following. At this rate, Longarm thought, and with any luck, he might catch up with Braddock the next day. It would have helped if he could ride all day, but the heat was too much around midday. The siesta was a necessity, not a luxury. He would never catch Braddock if the chestnut died under him.

Longarm figured he would also reach Presidio the next day. He had been to that border town a while back on another case. There were several saloons and whorehouses in Presidio. It was possible Braddock would stop there for a while if he was really as unconcerned about pursuit as he seemed to be. As Longarm made camp that night, he was convinced that he was closing in on his quarry.

He settled down in a cluster of boulders not far from the edge of the canyon, after first making sure there were no sidewinders lurking in the rocks. He had seen several of the deadly rattlesnakes during the trip upriver and had

20

taken pains to steer clear of them. It was enough to deal with human sidewinders like Braddock.

As always when he was on the trail, Longarm slept with one ear open. So when he heard a tiny cracking noise, he was instantly awake and alert. The sound had been like that of a branch breaking. The chestnut could have stepped on a fallen cedar branch, he thought—but so could someone else.

Longarm's breathing stayed regular. He gave no sign that he was awake. Anybody watching him would have thought him still asleep. Ever so slowly, he moved his hand closer to the butt of his gun. At the same time, his ears strained to hear any other sounds in the night. At the bottom of the canyon, the Rio Grande sang its bubbling, gurgling song, and a soft night breeze moved over the landscape with a sound like the sigh of a woman. Longarm heard nothing else.

Maybe he'd imagined the cracking noise, he told himself, but he discarded that thought even as it crossed his mind. He was too old a hand at this to make such a greenhorn mistake. Somebody or something had been moving around a minute earlier.

He smelled something then, and it wasn't the creosote bushes that grew nearby. Instead, it was the acrid tang of gun oil. A second after the scent drifted to his nose, he heard the unmistakable metallic sound of a cylinder revolving as somebody squeezed the trigger of a double-action revolver.

Longarm threw himself into a roll as a gun blasted almost right beside his head, half-deafening him. The bullet whined off a rock. As he rolled, he palmed out his Colt and lifted the gun as he came to a stop on his side. He'd seen the muzzle flash from the corner of his eye, so he had an idea where the gunman was. He triggered twice in that direction, then came up in a crouch and threw himself headlong behind a rock. A second bullet whipped past his head.

If the would-be killer had stood off a little farther and

21

emptied his pistol into Longarm, the big lawman wouldn't have had a chance. But it was a dark night, with the moon not up yet, and the gunman had wanted to make sure of his target. That extra bit of caution had backfired and saved Longarm's life instead.

Longarm knelt behind the boulder and waited to see what was going to happen. The edge of the canyon was at his back, so no one could get at him that way. On the other hand, he didn't have any place to retreat, either. If the mysterious gunman flanked him, he'd be a sitting duck.

Longarm's nerves stretched taut. After the shattering blast of the four shots, an eerie silence had descended over the darkness. He hated this sort of cat-and-mouse game, where the man who gave in and moved first was often the one who died. At the same time, waiting could play right into the other man's hands and give him the opportunity to improve his position if he could do it quietly enough.

The rattle of a rock moving sounded to Longarm's left. He pivoted in that direction, saw the looming figure, and fired. His bullets tore into the shape, which was little more than a deeper patch of darkness

Too late, he realized that the shape wasn't moving and that he had just blasted the hell out of a cholla cactus. At that moment, with a whisper of sound, a rope dropped over his head and settled around his upper arms, jerking tight. Longarm roared a curse and tried to turn so that he could bring his gun into play, but a hard tug on the rope sent him staggering to the side. He was dangerously close to the edge of the canyon, and he felt himself losing his balance. He fired the Colt wildly as another tug on the rope made his feet go out from under him.

He landed at the brink of the canyon and fought to stay there, but his weight tipped him over the edge. With the rope trailing behind him, he plummeted through the darkness toward the brawling river far below.

Chapter 3

The jolt as the rope halted Longarm's plunge felt like it broke at least two of his ribs. At the very least, it snatched all the air from his lungs, so he hung there for a second gasping for breath.

Then his arrested momentum swung him toward the face of the cliff and slammed him into the rock with stunning impact. Only half-conscious, he rebounded from the wall of the canyon and poised suspended at the end of the rope, his entire body revolving slowly. When the rope had twisted as far as it could go one way, Longarm's rotation stopped.

Then he started spinning back the other way.

Eventually the spinning stopped. He struggled mentally to gather his wits about him. His body was filled with pain. His feet dangled in nothingness. Despite the fact that he was a hardened lawman, a tiny voice far in the back of his brain gibbered in fear. He would not have been human had he not felt some crawling horror at the situation in which he found himself.

"Hey, down there!" a man's voice called from the rimrock. "You alive, hoss?"

Longarm groaned. Short of breath as he was, it was all he could manage.

The man on top of the canyon heard the sound. He shouted, "You just stay right there!" Then he laughed at the irony. Longarm couldn't do much of anything else except stay where he was.

The man must have moved back from the edge. After the echoes of his shout died away, silence filled the narrow canyon again. Longarm dragged as much air into his lungs as he could, constricted as he was by the rope around his chest and arms, so tight that it seemed to be cutting into his flesh through his shirt. Gradually, his muddled brain began to clear. The fierce anger he felt helped burn away the confusion.

He strained to tip his head back and look up. He estimated that he was about a hundred feet below the rim. After a fall like that, it was pure luck that his neck hadn't been broken when he was brought up short at the end of the rope. Longarm looked down but couldn't see anything except darkness. Only a little starlight penetrated into the canyon, not enough for him to be able to see the river.

In some places, the walls of Santa Elena Canyon rose a good fifteen hundred feet above the waters of the Rio Grande. Longarm didn't think the canyon was anywhere near that deep along this stretch. Still, there had to be at least a hundred feet of emptiness beneath him, maybe more. If he fell the rest of the way to the river, his chances for survival would be slim at best. True, there were pools down there that might be deep enough to break his fall, but there were also jagged rocks waiting to rend and smash.

No, Longarm decided, his best chances lay up, not down.

The rope hadn't settled exactly evenly around his torso when the son of a bitch up there on top lassoed him. It was cinched around Longarm at an angle, a little higher on the right side than on the left. Longarm began to wiggle a little, striving to drop his right shoulder. If he could

24

work that shoulder out of the lariat's loop, his right arm would be free. That might make the rope slide completely off him, leaving him to fall the rest of the way to the river, but if he moved quickly enough, he could reach above his head with his right hand and grab the rope, then hang on while he freed his left arm, and then with both hands free he could pull himself to the top . . .

Where he would likely find himself facing the gunman who had put him in this mess. But even so, Longarm knew he had to try. Otherwise, he would be at his enemy's mercy.

As he worked to get the rope off his right shoulder, he wondered if the man on the rimrock was Peter Braddock. It was possible. Braddock could have spotted someone trailing him and turned back to deal with the threat. Or the gunman could be some drifting owlhoot who just wanted to steal whatever Longarm had. Right now, the man's identity didn't really matter. What was important was getting out of this fix.

Longarm felt the rope slide a couple of inches higher on his right arm. He rolled his shoulder, and the rope moved another inch. He wiggled his fingers and flexed his elbow. His lower arm had grown a little numb from the pressure of the rope cutting off his circulation, but full feeling was returning to it now. Longarm welcomed the pins and needles as a good sign. He was able to lift his arm away from his body, and the rope slipped even more. It kept slipping, and suddenly it was off his shoulder.

Longarm lunged upward, reaching desperately with his right hand for the rope. His fingers brushed it, slid, then caught. His grip tightened like iron. He was holding on for dear life, literally.

After gathering his strength for a minute, he tried hoisting himself higher. Grunting with the effort, he pulled his weight up. With some slack on the loop at the end of the rope, he was able to wriggle out of it completely. His left arm was numb, just as the right one had been, but after a moment he had regained enough feeling so that he was able to reach up and grasp the rope with his left hand, too.

With the strain divided between both arms, it was a little easier to hold himself there. His shoulders were already beginning to ache, though, so he knew he couldn't stay like that indefinitely. After a few minutes of breathing deeply to replenish his oxygen-starved body, he began to think about pulling himself hand over hand to the top. If he could move upward even a yard or so, he could wrap his legs around the rope and split up the burden of supporting himself even more.

Longarm pulled. He hesitated, then let go with his right hand and reached up. Catching hold of the rope, he pulled again and let go with his left. It was all a matter of rhythm, he told himself as he kept climbing.

His actions made the rope sway, and he moved back and forth with it like a pendulum. Wildly, he thought about a story he'd once read by that fella Poe. On this stygian night, Santa Elena Canyon was a deep, dark pit, sure enough.

When he had pulled himself up far enough so that he could twist his legs around the rope, he stopped to rest. He was out of breath again from the effort, and his pulse hammered in his head.

"Hey! You still down there, Marshal?"

Longarm's head jerked back at the shout.

"I found your badge and your bona fides in your saddlebags," the man on the rimrock went on. "Deputy Marshal Custis Long. I've heard of you. You're the one they call Longarm."

Not saying anything, Longarm waited. Maybe if the bastard thought he was dead or unconscious, he'd go away, and then Longarm could finish his climb.

"I reckon they must've sent you after me. My name's Braddock."

Longarm's lips drew back from his teeth in a grimace, but still he didn't respond to the taunting shouts.

"You never would have got this close to me if my damn

horse hadn't gone lame," Braddock went on. "And then it happened again with the one I traded for in Lajitas! Can you beat that? Some fellas just have all the bad luck." He laughed again. "Of course, I'm the one up here and you're down there, so I reckon my luck's not all bad."

All Braddock had to do was tug on the rope to feel that Longarm's weight was still suspended from it, but it was so dark in the canyon that the fugitive wouldn't be able to tell that he was longer trapped in the loop at the end of the lariat. Go on! Longarm urged silently. Leave me here to die. Just get the hell out of here!

"When I spotted somebody on my back trail, I was afraid it might be some damned lawman," Braddock said. "Sure enough, I was right." An edge of anger crept into his voice. "You and all the others like you ruined a good thing for me down in Laredo, and now you figure to hound me for the rest of my life. Well, it won't do you any good, you hear me? None of you damn star packers will ever lay a hand on me!"

Braddock was wrong about that, Longarm thought. Even if he died, Billy Vail would just send somebody else after Braddock. And somebody else after that, if necessary, until finally justice caught up to the murderer.

"How about if I just drop you in this canyon, Long? How about that? I got this lasso snubbed around a tree up here, but all it'd take is a slash or two of my knife to cut it. What do you say?"

Longarm didn't say anything. Let Braddock think he was dead or unconscious. He wasn't going to give the son of a bitch the satisfaction of responding to the taunts.

Braddock must have been getting tired of gloating. He said, "All right, be that way if you want. I don't give a damn. Hate to lose a good rope, but I reckon you're at the end of it, Marshal."

Longarm's hands were closed tightly around the rope. Suddenly, he felt it vibrate slightly. The vibration continued, and Longarm realized to his horror that Braddock was making good on his threat. The fugitive was sawing through the rope.

The danger sent desperation coursing through Long-arm's veins. He started climbing again, faster this time, no longer being so careful. He pulled himself up as quickly as he could, knowing how slender the chance was that he could reach the top before Braddock cut the rope.

Braddock must have felt the rope jerking against his knife. Laughter pealed out from him. "Not playing possum anymore, are you, Long?" he cried. "Well, it's too late!"

Longarm had climbed ten or fifteen feet, but there was still well over fifty to go. He tilted his head back so that he could look up, and for the first time he caught a glimpse of his enemy. From this vantage point, Peter Braddock was nothing more than a dark shape at the edge of the rimrock, blotting out some of the stars that lay scattered across the black Texas sky. Longarm saw a tiny glint and knew it was starlight reflecting off the blade of the knife in Braddock's hand.

Longarm was still climbing when the rope parted, its tautness releasing with a sharp *twang!* At the same instant, Braddock shouted, "Go to hell, lawman!"

With a sickening feeling, Longarm fell straight toward the Rio Grande, the cut rope trailing after him.

It was a moment like no other Longarm had ever experienced. The seconds seemed to slow to a crawl, yet they were racing by at dizzying speed. He couldn't catch his breath, and he felt himself trying to black out. That was a part of his brain summoning him to blessed oblivion so that he wouldn't feel himself die, he supposed. But another part of his brain was still functioning with crystal clarity, and it was racing with the same speed that light raced through the heavens. The urgent signals it sent out transmitted themselves to Longarm's muscles, so that he brought his arms down and pressed them to his sides and held his legs tightly together. That seemed to make him fall even faster.

In the blink of an eye, he hit the water, boots first, and the impact rocketed up his body and exploded out the top of his head. That was what it felt like, anyway. A cold wet fist closed around him. His body had sliced cleanly into the fast-flowing river.

Longarm was aware that he was underwater, though it wasn't any darker than it had been before. He plunged deeper, expecting to feel himself crash into the bottom at any second. He was already running short of air. That shortage squeezed tightly at his chest. As he realized that he had stopped sinking without hitting bottom, something tangled around him, like thin, spidery arms that clutched at him and tried to hold him under the surface.

He kicked his feet and thrashed his arms, fighting off the entangling coils. The rope had fallen into the river with him, he realized, and that was what wrapped around his arms and legs. He struggled free of it and stroked for the surface. He hoped he was going in the right direction and hadn't gotten turned around.

His boots were holding him down. He stopped and fumbled with them, finally kicking them off his feet. Again he turned upward. The Rio Grande, fed by springs and snow melt from the distant mountains in New Mexico Territory, was cold even in the summer. The frigid water numbed his pains and cleared his mind even more.

He was alive! The fall hadn't killed him after all. Fate had guided him into one of those deep pools, and it had saved his life.

But unless he reached the surface and got some air soon, he was going to die anyway. His lungs felt like they were about to burst, and the blackness was now shot through with a red haze. Longarm knew that he had only a matter of moments, perhaps seconds, before he would be forced to take a breath and drown.

His head broke the surface as he gasped. He swallowed a little water, but mostly he gulped down fresh, life-giving

29

air. He coughed and choked, but he was breathing again. Nothing had ever been better.

But Longarm knew he was not out of danger. The current carried him along at a breakneck pace. The walls of the canyon slid past in a shadowy blur. Longarm had to fight to stay on the surface. The sheer speed at which he was traveling tried to force him down into the water.

Not only that, but there were rocks in the river. He banged against several small ones, luckily only glancing blows that spun him around. If he slammed head-on into one of the larger, more jagged rocks, the collision could easily dash his brains out.

His head went under. He came up sputtering and spitting water. Something nudged against his side. Longarm flailed at it, and his fingers brushed the rough surface of a tree branch. It darted away from him in the current.

The branch must have fallen from one of the cedars up on the rim. Longarm knew that if he could latch on to it, it would help support him in the madly racing water. He lunged toward where he thought the branch was, slapped only water, then tried again. This time he touched the branch again and grabbed it frantically before the current could snatch it away.

He tugged the branch closer and threw his other elbow over it. When he had both arms wrapped around it, he judged it to be three or four inches in diameter and more than two feet long. It was twisted and gnarled and jagged on one end where it had broken off the tree where it had grown.

Longarm held tightly to the branch and let the current sweep him along. He scraped and bounced past several more rocks. He had no idea how long he had been in the water. It seemed like hours, but he knew that couldn't be right. Still, as the current slowed a little and the canyon grew slightly wider, he thought he could see better. Faint gray light was seeping down from above. Dawn was on the way.

Longarm rested and let the cedar branch support him.

He might have been able to kick his way to one side or the other of the canyon, but that wouldn't do him any good. The rock walls rose sheer from the water with no paths, no handholds, no place to go. There were no beaches, only the walls of the canyon.

If he let himself be carried on downriver, sooner or later the canyon would end, and he would be able to crawl out of the water and collapse on the ground. He could do that, Longarm decided. He could ride the river to a better place. After all, he had survived for this long. His luck was not going to desert him now.

It was not long after that he heard the roaring of the rapids up ahead.

As the light grew stronger, he was able to see the rocks ahead of him and kick his way around them, steering the branch almost like he would have a boat. As the noise became louder, however, he peered ahead and saw the white water stretching all the way from one wall of Santa Elena Canyon to the other. The rapids filled the river, and there was no way around them.

He couldn't get out of the water, and he couldn't turn back. All he could do was go ahead and hope for the best.

The current increased, and suddenly he was among the rocks. Spray filled the air. The roar was like that of a giant beast. Longarm clung to the cedar branch and grunted as he slammed into rock after rock. He had thought that he was so numb from the coldness of the water that he couldn't feel any pain. He was wrong.

The rocks tore at him like fangs, pummeled him like clubs. He rolled over and found himself underwater, fighting his way back to the surface just in time to smash his right leg against one of the rocks. He cried out in agony, then sputtered and choked as water filled his mouth. He retched and twisted around, searching for air.

Only half-conscious now, Longarm forced everything out of his mind except a single thought: *Hang on to that branch.* The cedar branch was life and death to him. Without it, he would go under and stay under. With it, he still had a slim chance.

One more thought intruded itself into his brain: *Braddock*. He had to live, had to come through this so that he could catch up to Peter Braddock and teach the man what it meant to try to kill a United States deputy marshal. Longarm had never been a vindictive man, but right now his fire for vengeance on Braddock was so strong that he drew on it and felt it bolstering him. He couldn't allow himself to die until he had settled the score with that murderous son of a buck.

Longarm didn't know it when the rapids ran out and the water grew more calm, though the current was still fast. He was alive, but practically all of his senses had deserted him. He held on to the cedar branch and floated, letting the Rio Grande take him wherever it wanted to. He was in the hands of fate and the border river.

Gradually, awareness returned to him. He blinked his eyes and lifted his head, spitting out the water that had run into his mouth. He was in the deepest part of the canyon now. The stone walls towered high above him on each side. The watercourse was so narrow that he felt like he could reach out with either hand and touch the walls. The current was stronger again, rocketing him along. But thankfully, there didn't seem to be any rocks in this part of the river.

Longarm was wrong about that. He found out just how wrong a moment later when he crashed into a submerged boulder. The cedar branch was jolted out of his grasp. He cried out from the pain of the collision and from fear as the branch danced away from him on the current. He felt himself sinking and struggled to stay on top of the water. A frantic lunge brought him closer to the branch, but it was too far away now. He couldn't catch it.

Longarm went under. He kicked himself to the surface, gasped for air. Went down again, the icy water closing over his head. Here at the bottom of the deep canyon, it was almost as dark as night again. The morning sky

32

showed as a narrow strip of light, far, far above his head as he fought back to the surface once more.

"Braaaaaaaddock!" Longarm howled, the echoes of his cry reverberating from the canyon walls, bouncing back and forth until they sounded like some sort of insane chorus.

He fought to the last and never knew it when he lost consciousness.

The terrible, gut-wrenching sickness was the first thing he was aware of. He rolled onto his side and retched up what seemed like half of the Rio Grande. When the awful spasms finally stopped, Longarm flopped onto his back again and gasped for air.

"Senor? Senor, you are not dead?"

Longarm heard the voice as he became aware that he was lying on sand. Hot sand. And the sun was beating on his face. When he opened his eyes, the brightness was like daggers in them.

Something moved between him and the sun. A slender figure, topped by some sort of bulbous, grotesque protrusion. It took Longarm a moment of pained blinking to realize that he was looking up at a youngster wearing a broad-brimmed sombrero.

"You are not dead?" the boy asked again.

"N-not . . . hardly," Longarm said.

Then he closed his eyes and slipped back into the blessed darkness.

Chapter 4

Longarm smelled something when he woke up the second time. His nose wrinkled. When he had come west as a young man after the war, he had cowboyed enough so that he had an instinctive reaction to the smell of sheep, even now.

A moment later, he heard the woollies blatting. Somebody yelled at them in Spanish, the voice high and clear, a boy's voice.

Longarm opened his eyes, slitting them against the glare until they had adjusted somewhat. He rolled onto his right side, wincing at the pain that went through him as he moved. The worst of it was in his right leg. He remembered slamming that leg against a rock in the river. He hoped it wasn't broken. If it was, he would be laid up for a long time while it healed.

But eventually his leg *would* heal, and when that happened, he could get back on Peter Braddock's trail.

Braddock was going to be damned sorry that he had trusted to the river to kill Longarm.

A few yards away, a small campfire burned. Longarm smelled coffee and beans. His stomach twisted. He didn't know what was worse, the hunger that gripped him or the revulsion he felt when he thought about eating.

He looked past the fire along the beach. On the far side of the river, the stone wall of a cliff jutted up sharply, but on this side was a long, sandy beach that rose gradually, turning into a greasewood-dotted slope that led to a plateau. The sheep were scattered across that slope, grazing on *lechuguilla*, the lettuce-like plant that grew here in the Chihuahuan desert on both sides of the river. The boy Longarm had seen earlier was hazing the woollies down the slope toward the river, gathering them for the night.

Dusk was not far away, Longarm judged as he glanced up at the sky. That meant he had been unconscious most of the day. His clothes, soaked when he had come out of the river, were dry now, the moisture steamed out of them by the hot, dry air. He hitched himself up onto an elbow, then got his other hand underneath him and pushed up into a sitting position.

The boy noticed that he was sitting up and came running toward him. Longarm summoned a weak smile as the boy slid to a stop a dozen feet away and stood there staring at him. The boy carried a long pole with a crook in the end, a shepherd's staff.

"No, I ain't a ghost," Longarm said in English, since the boy had addressed him in that language earlier. "Are you the one who pulled me out of the river?"

The boy's head bobbed. "*Si*, senor," he said. "I see you come floating down the Rio Bravo and think that you are dead. But you are close enough so I can catch hold of you with this—" He hefted the pole. "So I pull you in to make sure."

"I'm much obliged," Longarm told him. "My name's Custis. What's yours?"

"I am called Pablo."

"Mighty pleased to make your acquaintance, Pablo," Longarm said. "Mighty pleased."

If Pablo hadn't pulled him out of the river, he would have surely drowned, Longarm thought. He owed the boy

35

his life. He would see to it that Pablo was rewarded for that.

Looking around at his surroundings again, Longarm went on, "We're on the Mexican side of the river, ain't we?"

"*Si,* that is Texas," Pablo said, waving at the cliff on the other side of the Rio Grande.

"I got to get back over there. Whereabouts are we?"

Pablo shook his head, evidently not understanding what Longarm was asking him.

"Which way is Presidio?" Longarm tried again.

Pablo waved a hand vaguely toward the northwest.

"What about Lajitas?"

A wave toward the southeast. That was about what Longarm figured. He was somewhere on the Mexican side of the river between Presidio and Lajitas. He had to get across the river, find a horse somewhere and a gun, and get back on Braddock's trail. He started climbing to his feet.

"Senor, no!" Pablo said. "You are hurt!"

"Got to get to Texas." Longarm reached his feet and stood there swaying unsteadily. His right leg throbbed like a bad tooth, but at least it supported his weight. It wasn't broken.

"How?" Pablo pointed at the sheer cliff on the other side of the river. "There is no crossing for many miles."

"Don't matter. I got to." Longarm turned. He would walk downriver to Paso Lajitas if he had to. He knew he could get across the river there.

He took one step and then his right leg folded up under him, throwing him forward on his face. He grunted and cursed as pain arrowed through him.

That leg might not be broken, but it didn't want to work right just yet. Well, by God, he'd crawl to Lajitas if he had to!

Pablo ran over and knelt beside him. "Senor, you must rest," the boy said. "You almost died. I will take you to

36

my *patron's rancho*. There are those there who will care for you—"

Longarm pulled away from the tentative hand Pablo placed on his shoulder. Every minute he delayed was one more minute that Peter Braddock was getting farther away. He didn't have time to lay around and recuperate. And he sure as hell didn't want Pablo taking him deeper into Mexico to some ranch.

"Sorry, kid," Longarm muttered as he struggled onto hands and knees. "I got to go—"

Everything wheeled crazily around him then, earth and sky changing places and revolving faster and faster until Longarm felt himself thrown clear off the world into a region of nothingness. His face smashed into something. He tasted sand in his mouth and tried to spit out the nasty, gritty stuff. Coughing and gagging, he rolled onto his back and realized that he had collapsed yet again. He stared up at the sky, conscious but unable to move, and watched as the sky turned purple and gold and dark, dark blue. The sun was setting behind the mountains to the west, and night was coming on.

Longarm passed out again, his last coherent thought not of his duty as a lawman or his thirst for vengeance on Peter Braddock but rather that the sky sure was pretty this evening.

When he came to again, somebody was punching him in the belly.

That was what it felt like, anyway. After a while he figured out he was lying facedown over the bony spine of some sort of critter that was plodding along slowly. His hands and feet were tied together under the animal's belly to keep him from falling off.

It had to be a mule he was on, Longarm thought. No other varmint had such a rough gait. He groaned and said, "Pablo?"

"Rest, senor," came the boy's reply from somewhere

37

up ahead, where he was leading the mule. "I will take care of you."

The way his sore belly was bouncing on the mule's spine, he was liable to die from Pablo's "care," Longarm thought. He lifted his head, forced his eyes open, saw the arid ground passing beneath him. They had to be on their way to that ranch Pablo had mentioned. Longarm groaned again. Instead of catching up to Braddock, he was getting farther away all the time.

"Is it morning again?" he asked.

"Si."

Longarm was about to ask the boy to cut him loose, so that he could at least ride upright on the mule, but before he could do that, he drifted off into the haze again. His body had absorbed too much punishment. He could stay awake for a while, but then everything started closing down around him.

There was no point in fighting it, Longarm realized as he slipped away into unconsciousness. The whole delay chafed at him, but he was lucky to be alive. He had to be grateful for that.

And the dark oblivion that enfolded him was so damned nice . . .

Shouting. Loud, exuberant yells in Spanish. That was what Longarm heard as awareness returned to him again.

He felt a jerk, and his hands and feet were suddenly free. Someone had just cut the bonds that had tied them together under the mule's belly.

Longarm slid off the back of the mule and would have fallen to the ground if a strong hand had not caught his arm. Another hand clapped him hard on the back, staggering him, but the grip on his arm held him up.

"Easy, *mi amigo*," a voice like thunder boomed. "You are hurt, no?"

"I am hurt, yes," Longarm grated between clenched teeth. After hanging over the mule's back for so long, his arms and legs were numb again. Feeling began to return to them, and as it did, Longarm looked over at the man who stood beside him.

He was almost as tall as Longarm, and his barrel chest and broad shoulders made him look massive. A mustache to rival Longarm's own swept out to the sides of his dark, rough-hewn face. A ponderous belly strained at the white shirt and charro jacket he wore. His trousers matched the jacket and were studded with conchas down the sides of the legs. A broad-brimmed sombrero was thumbed back on the vaquero's unruly thatch of black hair.

"They call me Diablito," the man said. "Little Devil, you know."

The man might be a devil for all Longarm knew, but there was nothing little about him. He wore two pistols tucked behind the red sash tied around his ample waist, and a sheathed Bowie knife was strapped to his right calf. Despite a certain buffoonish air about him, Longarm's instincts told him that the vaquero called Diablito was a dangerous man indeed.

"Pablo says you are a gringo who came floating down the river to the camp where he tends his sheep," Diablito went on. "He says that the Lord took pity on you and delivered you to us."

"Where are we?" Longarm asked.

"The valley of Las Hermanas del Fuego."

The Sisters of Fire. Longarm frowned as he translated the Spanish name. It didn't make any sense, he thought. But his brain was still too stunned to ponder it for very long.

The clatter of hoofbeats made him look around again. Several more vaqueros rode up. One of them, a tall, slender man in a black sombrero, had a grinning Pablo perched in front of him.

"Here is your savior now," Diablito said to Longarm. "How he got *un hombre muy grande* like you on his mule, I do not know."

Longarm didn't know, either, but he supposed he should be grateful to the boy. Pablo was only trying to do the right thing by taking the injured American to the ranch where his patron lived. Longarm wondered if Diablito owned the ranch. Probably not, he decided. The big vaquero wasn't dressed well enough to be the owner of a ranch.

"Now we will take you to the hacienda of Don Manuel Escobedo," Diablito said, confirming Longarm's guess. Don Manuel would be the patron of both Pablo and Diablito and these other vaqueros.

Maybe he needed to just stop arguing and go with these folks, Longarm decided. At the ranch of Don Manuel Escobedo, he would be able to borrow a horse or a wagon that would get him back to Lajitas. Escobedo might have a *curandero* around the ranch, too, somebody who had experience patching up the sort of cuts and bruises that seemed to cover Longarm's body. A few bandages and some liniment, and he'd be as good as new, he told himself. And maybe something to eat and drink.

"You got anything to ride besides that damned mule?" Longarm growled.

"You can ride double with Esteban," Diablito said, "though it will be slower than riding the burro. Not much slower, however."

"A horse sounds good to me."

Diablito led Longarm over to one of the riders. Longarm winced as sharp little rocks prodded the soles of his feet through his socks. His boots were now somewhere at the bottom of the Rio Grande, he thought, probably being nibbled on by fish.

Better his boots than his carcass, Longarm figured.

It didn't take him long to understand why the valley through which they rode bore the name it did. The peaks of the Sierra de Santa Elena surrounded the broad, deep valley, but the two mountains at the head of it dominated the landscape for miles around. Tall, steep-sided, and rugged, they loomed over the valley with their snow-capped crests seeming to reach halfway to heaven.

"Las Hermanas del Fuego," Diablito said, pointing to the mountains that were virtual twins. "We call them the Sisters of Fire because in times past the great cauldron of the earth has caused them to spew smoke and flames and the red lava so hot it can cook the flesh from a man's bones without ever touching him."

Longarm nodded. He rode behind the vaquero called Esteban, alongside Diablito. He knew that all the mountains in this region had been formed by volcanic action, most of it centuries in the past. From the looks of them, the Sisters of Fire were dormant, as were the others in the Sierra de Santa Elena chain. But there was no telling when the fires deep beneath the earth would rekindle themselves, and once again the molten rock would come boiling to the surface, searching for a place to erupt.

"The *rancho* of Don Manuel is called by the same name," Diablito went on. "It was during the time of his great-grandfather, old Don Estancio, that the Sisters of Fire last vomited up their brimstone. I have only heard stories of it, myself. Never have I been privileged to witness the mountains spit fire."

"No offense, old son," Longarm said, "but it'd be all right with me if I never saw such a thing."

Diablito threw back his head and laughed. "*Es verdad, mi amigo*, that those who have the best view of such a spectacle are usually those who are about to die."

They rode on, coming to a stream that flowed through the valley and turning to follow it toward the southwest. The valley curved, following the little river, and the towering dormant volcanoes were now on the right hand of the riders. The countryside grew more green, verdant with grass and trees. Longarm saw pines, junipers, and scrub oaks. Only miles away was arid desert fit only for cactus and lizards, but in these mountain highlands there was good grazing land. If this entire valley belonged to Don Manuel Escobedo, then his *rancho* was probably a successful one.

The vaqueros had given Longarm some water and tor-

41

tillas before they started for the hacienda, and while the food and drink had made him queasy for a while, he was glad now that he had taken some sustenance. He felt a little stronger, and he hadn't passed out for a while. That was always good. He was sure that Pablo had managed to get some food down him while he was senseless, otherwise he would have been even weaker.

Diablito rummaged in the *aparejos* attached to his silver-studded saddle and brought out a bottle of clear liquid. "Tequila?" he asked as he held out the bottle toward Longarm.

Longarm licked his lips. A bracer would be nice right about now, but at the same time, he worried about what the fiery liquor might do to him. He'd been passing out enough lately that he decided a few swigs of tequila might not be a good idea, no matter how tempting the offer was. He shook his head and said, "Thanks, but no thanks."

Diablito shrugged and pulled the cork in the bottle's neck with his teeth. He spat it into the hand holding his horse's reins, then lifted the bottle to his lips. The tequila gurgled loudly in the bottle as at least half of it vanished down Diablito's gullet. "Ahhhh!" he said as he lowered the bottle. He drove the cork back into the neck with the heel of his hand and stowed the bottle back in his saddlebags.

Longarm caught sight of some buildings up ahead. Nestled in a grove of trees was a sprawling adobe structure with several wings jutting out from the main house. Beyond the house were extensive corrals and two barns, as well as a long, low building of adobe that Longarm took to be the bunkhouse.

Gesturing toward the buildings with their red tile roofs, Diablito said, "The hacienda of Don Manuel Navarre Gonzalez y Escobedo. *Mi patron*. The finest man in all of Mexico."

Longarm hadn't met the gent, so he didn't know if Diablito's statement was true or not. He asked, "How far are we from the border?"

"Twenty miles, senor." Diablito frowned. "You are not still thinking about returning to Texas, are you, senor? You would not refuse the hospitality of Don Manuel?"

"I'll be glad to accept the don's hospitality," Longarm said, "but if that extends to the loan of a horse, I'd be much obliged."

"You must have very important business on the other side of the Rio Bravo," Diablito said, his frown deepening.

Longarm hadn't told any of them who he really was. His badge and identification papers were long gone. Probably Braddock had either taken them with him or thrown them into the river. Longarm didn't have any legal authority over here in Mexico anyway, so he figured he might as well act like a private citizen.

"I have business there, that's true," he told Diablito, and his tone made it clear that he didn't intend to discuss the matter any further, no matter how grateful he might be to his rescuers.

Diablito pushed out his heavy lips, tugged on his mustache, and said, "It is as you say, senor."

They rode on toward the hacienda. Someone must have seen them coming and spread the word, because several people emerged from the wrought-iron gate in the high adobe wall that ran around the outer courtyard. One of them was tall and slender, and his aristocratic bearing told Longarm he was probably Don Manuel Escobedo. As the group of riders came up to the hacienda and drew rein, the slender man lifted a hand in greeting.

"Hola, Diablito," the man said, then asked in rapid-fire Spanish who the stranger was.

"The river delivered him up to Pablo at the camp of the sheep," Diablito replied.

The slender man frowned. "From *el Rio Bravo?*"

"Si, patron."

The man came over to the horse where Longarm sat behind the vaquero called Esteban. "I am Don Manuel Escobedo," he said. He had thinning dark hair and a lean,

43

sensitive face. "Please accept the hospitality of my humble home."

There was nothing particularly humble about this hacienda, Longarm thought. In fact, it looked like a damned nice place. But he slid off the horse, gave Don Manuel a friendly nod, and said, "Much obliged, Don Manuel. If I might have the loan of a horse . . ."

"But you are injured!" Escobedo protested. "I saw the way you nearly fell when you dismounted. Your leg is hurt."

"Banged it on a rock in the river," Longarm said with a shrug. "I reckon it's just bruised."

"If you nearly drowned in the river, you will need to rest and recover your strength. I know just the person to take care of you." Escobedo turned to the three people who had accompanied him out of the house to meet the riders. One of them was an elderly man in dark livery, almost certainly a servant, as was the old woman who stood beside him with a shawl clutched tightly around her shoulders and over her gray hair. It was to the third person Escobedo spoke, saying, "Dulcey?"

This was a woman, too, in a shapeless gray dress with a hood pulled up so that it concealed her face. But as she stepped forward, Longarm saw that while the dress might be shapeless, the woman in it definitely wasn't. He recognized the lush curves of a well-built young woman. So it came as no surprise when she pushed back the hood and revealed a young, startlingly attractive face. Her cheekbones were high, indicating some Indian blood in her veins and setting off her dark eyes. A thick mass of curly, reddish-brown hair spilled from under the hood and fell around her shoulders. She was not classically beautiful or even particularly pretty, but she had about her an air of earthy sensuousness that could not be denied.

As the young woman stepped forward, Longarm saw from the corner of his eye that the boy Pablo was making a curious gesture. He didn't have time to think about it, because Don Manuel said, "Dulcey, you will care for our visitor and heal his injuries."

"*Si*, Don Manuel," she murmured in a throaty voice. She lifted an arm and held out a hand toward Longarm. "Come with me, senor."

Longarm hesitated, thinking that he ought to insist about borrowing a horse or a wagon so that he could get back to Lajitas. And a gun, he reminded himself. He needed a gun, too.

But then he looked in the eyes of the young woman called Dulcey, and he knew everything else would have to wait. Those dark eyes were so deep, so compelling, that Longarm couldn't bring himself to argue with her.

He took the hand she held out to him. Her fingers were smooth and cool and strong as they closed around his.

As she led him through the gate into the courtyard and toward the house beyond, he wondered fleetingly what there was about this lovely woman that had caused young Pablo to make the sign of the cross as she approached.

Chapter 5

The house was well-furnished, with woven rugs on the
floor and heavy, elaborately carved furniture. The thick
ceiling beams were visible, in the Spanish style. A huge
stone fireplace took up most of one wall in the main room.
Several sets of antlers were mounted on another wall, and
with them was a collection of obviously very old weapons: a long, wicked-looking dirk with a silver-filigreed hilt
and handle; a saber with a polished blade of Toledo steel;
a crossed pair of rapiers; and an ancient blunderbuss.
Longarm was curious about them and told himself that he
would ask Don Manuel about the collection when he got
the chance.

Right now, though, Dulcey took him through the main
room and down a corridor, through a door that led onto
a long gallery forming a U-shaped border around the
house's inner courtyard. A balcony with wrought-iron
railings overhung the gallery, supported by wooden pil-
lars.

"This will be your room," Dulcey told Longarm as she
led him by the hand to one of the rooms that opened off
the gallery. It had an arched wooden door. When Dulcey
swung it back, Longarm saw that the room was simply

furnished with a bed, a rug, a small table, and a chair. There was only one window, and it looked out on the stone fountain and the fruit trees and flower beds of the inner courtyard.

Longarm hesitated. Something about the room reminded him of a jail cell, of all things. But no jail cell he had ever seen had had a woman like Dulcey in it, beckoning him to join her.

He stepped inside, limping on his right leg. Dulcey said, "You must lie down, so that I can see to your injuries."

"You're a nurse?" Longarm asked her.

Dulcey's lips curved in a smile as she closed the door of the room. "I am one who knows how to soothe the hurts of the flesh—and the heart and soul."

Longarm was willing to bet that last part was true, anyway. He sat on the edge of the bed, and Dulcey knelt in front of him and slowly peeled his socks off his bruised feet. She rubbed his feet for a moment. It felt so good that Longarm had to close his eyes in pleasure as Dulcey's thumbs pressed hard into the soles of his feet and rotated in small circles.

Maybe she'd really meant "heart and *sole*," Longarm thought with a silent chuckle.

"Lie back," Dulcey said softly, and without even thinking about it, Longarm did as she told him. He stretched out on the mattress, unable to suppress a groan as he sank into its softness. His eyes were still closed. He felt Dulcey's fingers moving at the buckle of his belt and the buttons of his trousers. He knew he ought to object, but for some reason, he didn't.

She pulled his trousers down, then said, "Sit up for a moment." Longarm did so, and she peeled the torn and filthy shirt over his head and tossed it into the corner of the room where she had thrown his socks and trousers. He lay back again, clad only in the bottom half of a pair of long underwear. Dulcey took those off him, too, and he was naked.

47

To Longarm's surprise, there was nothing particularly arousing about the situation. As he lay there on the soft mattress, all the tension that had gripped him for the past few days seemed to evaporate, and the bruised and battered muscles of his body relaxed. For the first time, he truly felt all the punishment he had absorbed. Pain blossomed and grew inside him. He caught his breath.

"No," Dulcey murmured. Longarm felt the mattress move as she sat beside him. She said, "Surrender to what you feel. You must give the pain its due. Only then can you truly master it."

Longarm forced himself to lie still and breathe deeply. Maybe what Dulcey was saying would work. He hoped so, because right now he hurt like hell.

"Your right leg is bruised from your hip to below your knee," Dulcey went on quietly. "I do not think I have ever seen such a dark bruise." Her fingers probed his leg, and the pain spread outward. When she stopped, Longarm sighed in relief. "The bones are not broken. Your leg will heal." Her touch moved to his torso, the fingertips brushing him more lightly this time. "Here there are more bruises and many cuts. Wait."

Longarm wasn't sure where she thought he might be going. He didn't intend to move ever again unless a genuine howling calamity forced him to do so.

She got off the bed. He heard water splashing. There had been a pitcher and basin on the table, he recalled. A minute later Dulcey returned to sit next to him and begin washing his body with a cool, wet cloth.

The touch of it was wonderful. Dulcey gently cleaned away the dried blood from all his cuts and scratches. When she finished, she said, "I will be back."

Longarm was half-asleep by now. "Take your time," he slurred.

He wasn't sure if he drifted completely into slumber or not, but he was unaware of how much time had passed when he once again felt the touch of Dulcey's hands on his body. She began spreading something slick and wet over his flesh, but this time, instead of the coolness of the cloth, he felt heat growing as she massaged him. As the heat spread, the pain retreated from it.

Dulcey worked her way down his torso, and as her hands approached his groin, Longarm felt his manhood begin to stiffen. Drop him off a cliff, send him floating down the river and bouncing from rock to rock in the rapids, throw him belly-down over a mule . . . and still, after all that, the old boy started to get hard the first time a pretty gal got near it.

Well, it was good that there were some things in the world that a fella could depend on, Longarm thought.

Dulcey gave a low, throaty laugh. "I do not think you have healed quite that much so soon, senor."

"Sorry, ma'am," Longarm muttered. "Some things got a mind of their own."

"*De nada*. It is a good sign, a sign that you strive for life."

He felt bare flesh brush against his hip. Opening his eyes, he looked up and saw that Dulcey had removed her shapeless gray dress. She was nude, her heavy breasts with their dark brown tips hanging only a few inches from Longarm's face.

His shaft was fully at attention now, jutting up proudly from his groin. Dulcey laughed softly as she saw it throb. "That will make it difficult when I tell you to roll over on your belly so that I can rub this healing oil on your back."

"I'm sorry, but I don't rightly know what I can do about it," Longarm told her.

"Do not worry. I know what to do. But you must lie still. You must give me your word."

Longarm swallowed hard and nodded. "I'll be still," he promised.

Smiling, Dulcey moved her hands to his shaft. She wrapped her fingers around the thick pole and began to massage it. She still had enough of the oil on her hands so that Longarm felt the heat from the stuff. He began to breathe harder as exquisite sensations spread through him, centered on his manhood, but other than that he kept his promise and didn't move.

Dulcey stroked slowly up and down the shaft. "This is a muscle like any other," she said. "Sometimes a good massage is needed."

Time ceased to have any meaning. All that existed was this room and the two of them. Dulcey leaned over Longarm's groin, her head so close that he could feel the caress of her breath on the head of his shaft. He thought she was going to take it into her mouth, but instead she simply blew softly on it. That made the heat from the oil even hotter. He was on fire now, but he willingly surrendered to the flames. Dulcey milked clear fluid from the slit at the end of his organ and used her thumb to spread it slickly around the crown of flesh. Longarm's hips started to lift from the bed, as every instinct in his body told him to thrust with them.

"Be still," Dulcey whispered. "You must not move."

Longarm trembled as he forced his muscles to obey the woman's commands. She continued stroking and caressing, and the heat grew stronger and stronger . . .

She clasped one hand around his shaft and cupped the other around the head. "Give me your seed," she said, and Longarm's climax washed over him. He exploded like one of those long-dormant volcanoes, only the lava that erupted from him in spurt after soul-shattering spurt was thick and white, rather than red-hot. Longarm emptied himself, and Dulcey caught the liquid in her hand.

Then, like a woman drinking from a spring, she brought her cupped hand to her mouth and lapped up what he had given her, licking the last bit off her palm as Longarm watched in amazement, his heart still hammering wildly in his chest.

Dulcey turned and leaned over him, smiling down into his eyes. "You are a strong man," she whispered. "You will be well soon."

"Dulcey . . ."

"Dulcinea. My true name." Her tone became more impersonal. "Now you can roll over so that I can spread the oil on your back, no?"

Longarm rolled over, and Dulcey continued the massage. Sometime during it, Longarm fell sound asleep, and his last thought was her name.

Dulcinea.

The next week passed in a daze for Longarm. He spent most of it in the small room off the gallery. Dulcey brought him his meals there. He slept for long hours each day, and when he was awake, she was with him, massaging away the aches and pains from his injuries. He could feel himself healing, and with his own eyes he could see that the bruises on his body were growing smaller each day. It hardly seemed possible that they could fade so quickly, but they did.

He and Dulcey talked as well, and he learned that she had been born in Spain, rather than Mexico. Her father had been a soldier and had come to Mexico in 1864, when Maximilian seized control of the country aided by Napoléon III's French troops and declared himself Emperor. As a general in Maximilian's army, the fall of the so-called Empire had meant death for Dulcey's father, and that had left Dulcey and her mother to fend for themselves in a suddenly hostile country.

"My mother left me with people who had been our servants," Dulcey said quietly as she and Longarm sat on the bed and rays of sunlight slanted in through the window. Outside in the courtyard, the waters of the fountain danced and laughed. "I never saw her again. The couple who raised me were kind in their way. They were servants, so I became a servant. The woman was an *Indio*. I learned much from her."

Longarm wasn't quite sure what she meant by that, but she didn't seem inclined to go on, so he didn't press the issue.

"I worked in the house of Don Manuel in Mexico City,

51

and when his father died and Don Manuel came here to run this *rancho*, I came with him."

"He seems like a good hombre."

"He is a fine man. Perhaps too fine." Dulcey looked away. "Fine men are sometimes weak. They lack the tempering in flame that those who are not so fine have received."

Longarm didn't know what that meant, either, but he wasn't worried about it. In fact, he wasn't worried about anything. Whenever Dulcey wasn't with him, he slept, a deep, dreamless slumber that allowed all the cares of his body and soul to knit themselves together again. And when she was with him, he thought of nothing else except her. Her beauty, her gentle touch, her soft laughter. . . . It seemed incredible, but as he had healed, she had grown more lovely. With each passing day, he thought she was the most beautiful woman he had ever seen.

If anyone had asked him how he had come here to Las Hermanas del Fuego, Longarm could have told them. He remembered his pursuit of Peter Braddock, remembered the way the fugitive had bushwhacked him and dropped him off the cliff into the Rio Grande to die. There was nothing wrong with his memory.

But whenever Dulcey was around, he just didn't think of those things.

Longarm walked gingerly across the inner courtyard toward the fountain, using a cane to ease the strain on his right leg. Don Manuel sat there in a heavy chair, along with Diablito, his *segundo* and the man in charge of everyday operations on the ranch. Dulcey was there, too, perched on a low stool beside Don Manuel's chair, and in the background hovered the servant woman Longarm had seen on his first day at the ranch, but not since then.

Diablito hailed him. "Custis, *mi amigo*! How is it you feel?"

Longarm stopped and leaned his weight on the cane. "Not bad, I reckon," he said.

Don Manuel smiled. "You were very, how do you Americans say it, banged up?"

"One should never run the rapids of the Rio Bravo without a sturdy boat!" Diablito said with a laugh.

Longarm lowered himself carefully into an empty chair next to the two men. "Can't argue with that," he said. "I'd just as soon never run those rapids again, even in a boat."

"Dulcey says that you will be able to travel in another week, perhaps two," Don Manuel said.

Longarm frowned. He had come out here on this late afternoon to say something, and he was determined to get it out. But what in blazes was it? He couldn't seem to remember . . .

Traveling, that was it. Longarm was glad Don Manuel had brought up the subject. Forcing himself to concentrate, he said, "I can't wait that long."

"What? I do not understand, senor."

"I can't wait that long," Longarm said again. "I surely do appreciate everything you've done for me, Don Manuel, but I got to be getting back across the border." He had a job to do, a voice in the back of his head was saying. A fugitive to track down.

Escobedo sat forward in his chair, a worried look on his thin, clean-shaven face. "I think that is a bad idea, Custis. Your injuries have barely begun to heal—"

"I'm all right," Longarm cut in, not wanting to be rude but knowing that he couldn't allow himself to listen to Don Manuel's arguments. If he did, he would find himself persuaded to stay here at the ranch. He was certain of that. "The bruises have all gone away, and I don't really need this cane." He stood up, using the cane to brace himself, then let go of it and allowed it to fall to the ground. He began to walk around the fountain. "See? I'm just fine."

Other than feeling as weak as a damned kitten, he thought. But that weakness would only go away if he got up and started moving around again, doing things, going about his business.

53

And his business was tracking down Peter Braddock and bringing him to justice. There was no way Longarm could do that as long as he was lazing around this *rancho*, as pleasant as life here was as it flowed sweetly from day to day.

Longarm had his back to the others momentarily as he walked along beside the low stone wall around the fountain. As he stopped and turned toward them, he saw Don Manuel looking intently at Dulcey, as if waiting for her to tell him what to do. Longarm thought he even caught a glimpse of Dulcey shaking her head. Then Don Manuel looked at him again and said, "I cannot allow it, my friend. To let you leave now would be a grave mistake. My sense of hospitality insists that you remain with us until you are fully healed."

Don Manuel was just trying to be a good host, Longarm told himself. He didn't want to offend the man. Surely another week or two wouldn't hurt anything. . . .

Longarm stiffened and gave a little shake of his head. There he went again, going along with what somebody else was telling him to do, just because it would be the easiest and most pleasant course. He had to stop doing that.

"I'm sorry, Don Manuel," he said. "I don't have any choice."

"One always has choices," Escobedo snapped.

"Not this time. I'll walk to Texas if I have to."

Don Manuel drew in a deep breath, then let it out in a sigh. "Very well. If you insist on leaving us, Custis, we cannot keep you here. But I believe this to be a bad thing."

"Sorry," Longarm said again.

"You will have a horse, of course. The finest mount from my remuda. And some of my vaqueros will ride with you to the border." Don Manuel made a small gesture with his hand. "This country, it is sometimes not safe for a man riding alone. There are mountain lions—and other dangers."

"I'm obliged for the help."

"It is nothing." Don Manuel stood up. "You will join me for dinner tonight?"

"I'd be honored," Longarm said.

Don Manuel nodded and turned to walk back into the hacienda. Diablito followed him, and so did Dulcey, but the young woman hesitated for a moment, her gaze on Longarm's face. In the growing dusk, he couldn't read her expression. He had the feeling that even if he could have seen her face plainly, he wouldn't have been able to tell what she was thinking.

Chapter 6

The atmosphere at dinner was a bit strained, but not too bad considering that Don Manuel could have taken even more offense at the insult to his hospitality, Longarm decided. The man was formal in his speech but not unfriendly.

"Tomorrow morning, you will have your pick of my horses," Don Manuel said.

"I'll see that you get it back."

Don Manuel waved a hand carelessly. "Fine horses can always be bred. Keep it as my gift to you."

"Thank you," Longarm said sincerely, not wanting to make things worse by refusing anything else.

He and Don Manuel ate alone. There was no sign of Dulcey. The elderly couple served the dinner. Longarm wondered where Dulcey was. As a servant, it made sense that she wouldn't sit down to eat with the owner of the hacienda, but for some reason Longarm had thought she might be here. She wasn't a typical servant.

For one thing, that afternoon he had gotten the impression that it was really Dulcey who gave the orders around here, not Don Manuel. Longarm was sure he had seen Escobedo looking to Dulcey for guidance, as if he were depending on her to do the thinking for him. After all, it had been Dulcey who had said that Longarm would be ready to travel in another week or two, rather than right away. Don Manuel had taken his cue from her on that matter.

Longarm sipped his wine and wondered if Don Manuel depended on Dulcey for other things. If Don Manuel had a wife, Longarm had seen or heard nothing about her. He suspected the *ranchero* was unmarried. Even if Don Manuel did have a wife back in Mexico City or somewhere else, Dulcey could still be warming his blankets at night. It sure as hell wouldn't be the first time a master had bedded one of his servants, Longarm thought.

There had been no repeat of what had happened between Longarm and Dulcey on his first day at the ranch, but he certainly hadn't forgotten about it. If Dulcey was performing similar tricks in Don Manuel's bed, it was no wonder the man didn't want to cross her. She might be a servant, but it was possible she was the real mistress of this household.

It was a good thing he was getting out of here now, Longarm told himself as he ate the spicy roasted chicken and the vegetables on the plate in front of him and washed them down with more wine.

Otherwise he might never leave Las Hermanas del Fuego.

Longarm felt stronger than he had in a week as he walked back to his room that night. He'd had brandy and cigars with Don Manuel after dinner, and while Longarm would have enjoyed some Maryland rye and one of his own cheroots even more, the evening had passed very pleasantly. They had talked about the collection of antique weapons hanging on the walls, and Don Manuel explained that they had come down to him from Don Estancio Escobedo, his great-grandfather and the first man to settle in the valley of the Sisters of Fire.

Longarm had left the cane in his room, convinced that

57

he no longer needed it. His right leg was still sore and a little stiff, but he was able to walk without a limp. The strength that had been missing in his limbs earlier today was returning gradually. Riding twenty miles to the border wasn't going to be a picnic, but Longarm was confident that he could do it.

A couple of lanterns burned in the fruit trees in the inner courtyard, but otherwise the place was in darkness except for starlight. Longarm could see well enough to find the door of his room with no trouble. He lifted the latch string, swung the door open, and stepped inside.

Instantly, something warned him that he wasn't alone.

He moved aside quickly from the door so that he wouldn't be silhouetted against the light from outside. Pressing his back against the adobe wall beside the window, he waited, silent and motionless, his keen ears intent for the slightest sound that might warn him of an enemy's presence.

He had a habit when he stayed in hotels of wedging a matchstick between the door and the jamb, down low where an intruder wouldn't notice it. If the match had been disturbed when he returned to his room, he would know that someone had been there, might still be there. In that case, he usually went in with his gun drawn and ready.

Here at the hacienda of Don Manuel Escobedo, he didn't have any lucifers, and even if he had, he probably wouldn't have thought of putting one of them in the door. That would have required too much effort.

He didn't have a gun, either. In fact, he was unarmed. He wished he had taken the cane with him after all. At least he could have used it as a club.

Suddenly, he saw motion in the light that came in through the door and spilled across the bottom third of the bed. A smooth, bare, coppery female leg stretched across it. Longarm heard a faint chuckle, then Dulcey said, "Close the door, *por favor,* Custis."

Longarm started breathing again. He reached over,

found the door, and pushed it shut. "I didn't expect to find you here, Dulcey," he said.

"If you are so foolish as to leave the ranch, I will never see you again, Custis."

"You don't know that." Longarm moved closer to the bed. He had spent so much time in this room, he didn't need light to know his way around. A little illumination filtered around the curtains over the window, but not much. "I might just ride back this way sometime."

"My head tells me this is so, but my heart tells me it will not happen."

Longarm lowered himself onto the bed beside her. "Well, then, we have tonight, I reckon. We'd better make the best of it."

Dulcey sat up and her arms went around his neck. "That is what I was thinking . . ."

Their mouths found each other and locked together in an urgent kiss. Longarm's tongue darted against Dulcey's lips, and they parted in invitation. He explored the warm, wet cavern of her mouth as he drew her closer and found that as he expected, she was nude. He cupped her left breast, feeling the nipple harden against his palm.

Dulcey took hold of his other hand and brought it between her legs so that he could feel her wetness. He rubbed her mound, then slipped a finger into her slickness. His thumb prodded the sensitive little nubbin at the top of her opening. Dulcey's hips jerked back and forth, and she moaned in passion against Longarm's mouth.

His shaft was already as hard as an iron bar. He wasn't going to be satisfied with what she had done to him last time. Then he had been so battered and exhausted there was nothing else he could do. Tonight, he felt new energy flowing through him, and he knew he was going to release it inside her.

Her fingers fumbled with the buttons of the shirt he had borrowed from one of the vaqueros. She stripped it back and ran her fingers through the mat of dark brown hair on his broad chest. She pulled her lips away from his and gasped, "Lie down, Custis! I want to ride you, my stallion!"

Longarm was glad it was dark in the room right then, because he couldn't help but grin at what Dulcey said.

Then it was time to get down to serious business. He got out of his borrowed clothes and boots as fast as he could, tossing them helter-skelter across the room. He sprawled on his back on the soft mattress, and Dulcey swung a leg across his hips and poised above him. She grasped his shaft, ready to lower herself onto the thick pole of male flesh. Before she sheathed him inside her, however, she paused and said, "You must let me do all the work, Custis. You are still weak."

Longarm just grunted. He didn't want to waste time arguing with her now.

Dulcey sank down slowly. Longarm felt the tip of his shaft touch the folds of soft, damp flesh. Her opening spread around his organ, gradually engulfing it. After a maddening moment, she had him all the way inside her, her bottom resting against the heavy sacs below his shaft.

Dulcey let out a long sigh and sat there like that for a while, obviously enjoying the fullness of having him inside her. Then her hips began to pump, slowly at first and then faster. Longarm reached up and caressed her breasts, pulling gently on the erect nipples, and that made the pace of Dulcey's thrusting increase even more.

Suddenly, a wave of contrariness swept over Longarm. Dulcey wanted him to just lie there and let her have her way with him. She was used to being in charge, and that was fine—part of the time. But since Longarm had gotten his strength back, letting her completely take the initiative rubbed him the wrong way.

He moved his hand from her breasts to her hips and grasped them tightly. Making sure that he was buried snugly inside her, his muscles tensed.

"Custis?" Dulcey exclaimed, sounding alarmed. "What are you—"

Longarm rolled over, holding her tightly against him

so that they were fully joined. Dulcey cried out, "Custis, no!" But she wound up on the bottom anyway. Longarm poised his hips between her widespread thighs and began some thrusting of his own, driving his manhood in and out of her.

He felt incredibly strong. Power surged through him. Dulcey clasped her arms around his neck and panted passionately against his ear as he made love to her. Longarm slid his hands underneath her and cupped her bottom, lifting her so that he could penetrate her even more fully. She pulled her knees up and threw her legs over his shoulders.

"*Dios mio!*" she moaned. "You are splitting me apart, Custis! Don't stop!"

Longarm pounded into her again and again, taking her hard and fast. His climax boiled up so quickly that it took him by surprise, and he couldn't hold it back. It didn't matter, because Dulcey was already thrashing and screaming in the culmination of her own passion.

Longarm spasmed, flooding her core with his fluids. They mixed with her own juices and overflowed, soaking them both. Longarm collapsed on top of her, pressing her into the mattress with his weight. She embraced him, kissing his nose and cheeks and lips.

Then, she said in a slightly chiding tone of voice, "You should have done as I told you."

For his answer, Longarm gave a twitch of his hips, sliding his still-erect organ deeper into her. Dulcey gasped and then made a noise of contentment deep in her throat.

Longarm rolled off her and lay beside her for a moment, holding her. The burst of strength and vigor that had gone through him earlier had faded, but he still felt all right. He was more convinced than ever that he was recovered from his injuries.

A slight sound from outside made him stiffen. Had that been the scuff of a footstep on the stone floor of the gallery? Longarm let go of Dulcey and swung his legs off the bed, standing up quickly.

"Custis—?"

"Shhh." Longarm catfooted to the window and flicked the curtain aside. Nothing was moving in the courtyard. He stepped over to the door and opened it a few inches, just enough to look out. No one was there. There was no evidence that anyone had been there.

But Longarm's gut told him that someone had. The adobe walls and the wooden doors of the hacienda were quite thick, thick enough to muffle most sounds. But the way Dulcey had cried out when she reached her climax, anyone who was passing by outside on the gallery would have been able to hear her. Had there been someone out there? Had they paused to listen, hearing what was going on inside?

Had it been Don Manuel Escobedo?

Longarm didn't know the answers to those questions, but he was frowning as he came back to the bed. That uncertainty was one more reason it was a good thing he was leaving the ranch and heading back across the border.

He heard Dulcey moving around. "What are you doing?" he asked.

"Getting dressed."

"You're not staying?" Longarm asked in surprise.

"It is not my place."

"You don't have to go," he told her. "Not as far as I'm concerned."

"Yes, I must." She came to him in the darkness, and as he took her in his arms, he felt that she had pulled on her dress. She kissed him quickly. "Adios, Custis."

"I'll see you in the morning. We can say good-bye then."

"No. Tonight . . . this was our farewell." The tone of her voice made it clear that she wouldn't stand for any argument.

"Whatever you want," he said quietly. "I ain't likely to forget you anytime soon, Dulcey."

"My name," she whispered. "Say my true name."

"Dulcinea." Longarm repeated it. "Dulcinea . . ."

Then she was gone, slipping from his arms like a wraith. He barely heard the door opening and closing. His arms were empty.

He had never felt quite so lost and alone in his life.

Longarm spent a restless night, finally dozing off in the wee hours. He was awake again before dawn, and when it became obvious to him that he wasn't going back to sleep, he rattled his hocks out of bed and got dressed. A look out the window told him it was growing light, so he knew people would be up and about on the ranch. Don Manuel had told him he could have his pick of the horses in the remuda. Longarm decided to mosey on over to the corrals and have a look at them.

He stepped out into the courtyard. It was quiet and peaceful this early in the morning, but he heard voices floating on the air. The vaqueros were getting ready to ride out on their day's chores. Longarm followed a flagstone path to a gate at the rear of the courtyard. The gate opened on a tunnel that led through a wing of the hacienda to another gate. That one went outside.

Longarm enjoyed the coolness of the morning air as he walked across to the corrals. As he passed one of the barns, someone called to him, "Senor Custis!"

Longarm turned toward the open door of the barn as the boy named Pablo hurried out. Pablo skidded to a stop, jerked his floppy-brimmed sombrero from his head, and bowed.

"Shoot, you don't have to do that, old son," Longarm told him with a grin. "I ain't your *patron*."

"You are an honored guest of Don Manuel," Pablo replied. "Therefore, I must honor you as well."

"I reckon you already did that by saving my life." Longarm stepped over to the boy and put his hand on Pablo's shoulder. "What're you doing here? I figured you'd be out at that sheep camp by the river."

Pablo finally looked up at him again. "One of the other boys is watching the sheep. We take turns."

"Well, it's good that you get to come back here to the hacienda sometimes, I guess. Why don't you walk on over to the corrals with me? Don Manuel said I could have a horse. Maybe you can help me pick it out."

Pablo put his sombrero on and fell in step beside Longarm, hurrying to keep up with the rangy lawman's long strides. "You are leaving Las Hermanas del Fuego?"

"That's right. Like I told you by the river, I got to get back on the American side."

"This is a good thing," Pablo said solemnly. "Soon there will be much trouble here."

Longarm stopped walking, and Pablo did likewise. Frowning down at the boy, Longarm repeated, "Trouble? What do you mean by trouble?"

Pablo looked up at him, dark eyes bright under the brim of the sombrero. "Shooting. Killing."

That answer just deepened Longarm's puzzlement. He said, "Hold on a minute. Let's eat this apple one bite at a time. I thought this *rancho* was a pretty peaceful place. Who'd want to go around shooting and killing?"

"The men of El Gordo." Pablo practically spat as he said the name.

"The fat one?" Longarm translated.

"*Si*. Though he is not so fat. But so he calls himself. Gordo Harrigan."

"Who in blazes is that? A bandit?" At times, the mountains of northern Mexico were thick with desperadoes, Longarm knew.

Pablo shook his head. "He may have been a bandit once, I do not know. But now he owns the *rancho* on the other side of the ridge that runs south of the Sisters. And he hates Don Manuel."

Longarm was beginning to understand now. The rivalry between neighboring ranches could get pretty ugly, especially if they were fighting over grass or water or both. He had seen more than his share of bloody range wars north of the border. There was no reason to think such things could not take place down here below the Rio Grande.

He nodded. "Like two dogs with one bone, eh? What are they squabbling over, grazing land or a creek?"

Pablo shook his head. "Neither, senor. They fight over Senorita Theresa."

That threw Longarm for a loop again. Who was Senorita Theresa? He hadn't heard that name since he'd been here on Escobedo's ranch.

"I don't reckon I know what you're talking about," he said to Pablo.

"Senorita Theresa is Don Manuel's sister. She is very beautiful, and Gordo Harrigan plans to marry her."

"Where is she? I haven't seen her around here."

"That is because she is at El Gordo's ranch. She has gone there to stay with him, even though they have not been married by a priest." Pablo looked and sounded older than his years as he added, "This dishonor has made Don Manuel very sad and very angry. He would like to kill Gordo Harrigan, I think. And Gordo Harrigan would like to kill him."

Longarm rubbed his jaw. If that didn't beat all. He'd been around the ranch for a week, and he'd had no idea there were such troubling undercurrents going on. But he supposed that was understandable, since he'd been laid up and sleeping a lot of that time. He'd had no reason to delve into Don Manuel's personal problems.

He still didn't, he reminded himself. His job was to bring Peter Braddock to justice, not to sort out the troubles of these folks down here in Mexico.

"I'm sorry to hear about that," Longarm said to Pablo. "I hope things work out all right for Don Manuel."

"I pray to the Blessed Virgin every night that this will be so," Pablo said. "But you see now why I am glad you are leaving, Senor Custis. If you stayed, you might be hurt, and this is not your fight."

Longarm felt a twinge of guilt. Pablo had saved his life, after all, and Don Manuel had opened his home to him.

Dulcey had nursed him back to health. No matter how you looked at it, he owed these people a debt, and he wished he could repay it by helping them.

But the debt he owed to Uncle Sam and the United States Justice Department was even bigger. The job had to come first, before any personal considerations. Longarm had known and understood that ever since the first time he'd pinned on a lawman's badge.

"Let's find that horse," he said with a sigh as he turned once more toward the corrals.

As he and Pablo walked along, Longarm added, "If you see Dulcey, you reckon you could tell her—"

He stopped short as he saw the boy cross himself. Longarm looked down at Pablo and asked, "What the heck is that all about? How come you make the sign of the cross just at the mention of Dulcey's name?"

Pablo did it again and said in all seriousness, "To protect my soul, senor. Because the woman of whom you speak, she is a *bruja*. What you call a witch."

Chapter 7

Longarm stared at the boy, not sure if his ears had heard correctly what Pablo had said. Pablo calmly returned the look, and Longarm knew that he'd heard right. And he knew that Pablo firmly believed what he had just said.

"A witch," Longarm repeated heavily.

"*Si*, senor. She has made a pact with Satan, that one."

Longarm didn't believe that for a second, no matter what Pablo said. He didn't believe in witches, although awhile back he had run across a couple of gals up in Wyoming who had made him wonder for a while if he was wrong. But even if those two *had* been witches, they had been the good kind, not the sort of evil creature Pablo was describing.

Pablo must have seen the doubt on Longarm's face, because he said, "You do not think I speak the truth, Senor Custis?"

"I reckon you're telling what you think is the truth," Longarm said. "I'm just too old and hardheaded to go believing in such things."

Pablo shrugged. "You have fallen under her spell, too, just like Don Manuel."

Longarm felt a flash of anger. No matter how much he

liked the boy, he wasn't going to stand there and listen to him bad-mouth Dulcey. He jerked his head toward the corrals and said, "Come on."

"No, senor," Pablo said with a shake of his head. "You must walk your own path. But as I said, I am glad you are leaving Las Hermanas del Fuego. You will be better off in your own land."

Before Longarm could say anything else, Pablo turned and ran off toward the barn. Longarm frowned as he watched the boy go, then with a grimace he turned toward the corrals again. When he'd climbed out of bed this morning, all he'd had on his mind was picking out a horse and leaving the ranch. Pablo sure had dumped a load of fresh worries on his head.

Diablito stood by the nearest corral. The burly *segundo* greeted Longarm with a grin and an upraised hand. "*Buenas dias*, Custis. You have come to pick out a horse?"

Longarm nodded. "That's right. Will you be riding up to the Rio with me, Diablito?"

"Sad to say, no. I must tend to my duties here on the ranch. But Esteban and three more of the men will accompany you and make sure you reach the border safely."

"I'm much obliged for that."

"*De nada.*" Diablito's grin flashed again. "The *ladrones* will not have to fear the scourge of my words today."

So riding with the wayward gringo to the border was pretty much a holiday for Esteban and the others, eh, Longarm thought. That was all right with him.

With a wave of a big hand, Diablito indicated the horses in the corral. "There are some of the finest mounts in all of Mexico," he declared. "Which one would you have as your own, Custis?"

Longarm leaned on the sturdy fence surrounding the corral and studied the animals. After a moment, he pointed to one of them and said, "What about that big roan?"

Diablito shook his head. "He has a hard mouth. You would not want him."

Longarm accepted the advice with a nod. "All right, what about the black with the white blaze?"

"Ah, what a rough gait that one has!" Diablito looked up at the sky and shook his head. "A man's tailbone would ache for days after riding that one a mile."

"Unh-huh," Longarm said. He was beginning to understand now. Diablito might praise the remuda to high heaven when he was speaking of them in general, but he was going to find fault with whatever horse Longarm picked until he happened to hit on the one that Diablito wanted him to have. It would probably save time just to ask. "Which one do you think is the best?"

Diablito squinted one eye and pointed. "You see that one there?"

"The mouse-colored one with the dark stripe down its back? The ugly one?"

"Ugly?" Diablito boomed, sounding mortally offended. "*Dios mio*, that is a lineback dun! The breed that never dies!"

Longarm grinned. "I'm joshing you, pard. I've ridden duns before. They're good hosses, and if you vouch for that one, I'll be glad to take it."

Diablito clapped a hand on his shoulder. "You will not be sorry, *mi amigo!*" He called to one of the vaqueros hanging around the corral to saddle the horse.

While that was going on, Don Manuel walked up to Longarm and Diablito. The rancher's face was taut, and in the growing light, Longarm thought he saw a flicker of hostility in the eyes of Don Manuel.

Longarm thought about what had happened the night before. He was still convinced that someone had been lurking outside his room while he was making love to Dulcey. Who was more likely to have been skulking around the hacienda than the man who owned it?

"*Buenos dias*, senor," Don Manuel said with a curt nod. "You have selected a horse?"

69

No matter how offended Escobedo might be by what had happened between Longarm and Dulcey, if that was actually the case, he wasn't going to withdraw an offer already made, Longarm thought.

"That lineback dun being saddled," Longarm told the rancher. "And I appreciate it, Don Manuel."

"You are most welcome," Don Manuel said, but he didn't sound very sincere. "I know how anxious you are to reach the border and return to your own land, so I had the cook prepare food for you to take with you." He gestured sharply to the elderly male servant, who had followed him from the hacienda. "That way you can leave even sooner."

Yep, Don Manuel was jealous, all right, Longarm told himself. He wasn't going to sit down for even one more meal with the *norteamericano* who had shown up uninvited on the ranch and bedded the gal who Don Manuel obviously considered his private property. It was a shame that things had turned out this way, but Escobedo was right: the sooner Longarm headed for the Rio Grande, the better.

"Much obliged," Longarm said as he took the bag of food from the servant. "I reckon now there's nothing keeping me here."

"One more thing." Don Manuel held out a coiled shell belt and holstered Colt. Longarm saw that the rig was his own, but the revolver was new, not the one he had dropped in the river and lost.

Longarm took the belt and buckled it on. The weight of the gun felt damned good on his hip. For the first time in quite a while, he realized just how naked he had felt when he wasn't packing iron.

"Thank you, Don Manuel, for your gracious hospitality," Longarm said as he extended a hand to the rancher.

Escobedo hesitated, but his sense of honor would not allow him to ignore Longarm's hand. He took it in a brief, firm handshake. *"Vaya con Dios,"* he said.

"And you, too," Longarm replied. *"Vaya con Dios."*

He turned away, and Diablito was waiting for him. The big vaquero swept Longarm into a bear hug and pounded him on the back, nearly knocking the breath out of him. "Farewell, my friend," he rumbled.

Longarm returned the backslapping. "So long, *amigo*."

One of the other men led the dun up. Longarm saw that the vaquero called Esteban and three other men were already mounted and ready to ride. He took the dun's reins, grasped the saddle horn, and swung up into the saddle. When he was set, he tied the bag of food onto the horn, then lifted a hand in farewell.

Diablito returned the wave. Don Manuel did not. Longarm glanced at the hacienda as he rode past, thinking that he might see Dulcey peering out from one of the windows or gates, but there was no sign of her. She had said her good-byes to Longarm the night before, and she was sticking to that resolve.

He sighed, knowing that he was riding away from the ranch—and from Dulcey—probably for the last time. He thought of the troubles Pablo had told him about and hoped sincerely that they wouldn't come down to a shooting war with that hombre Gordo Harrigan. He hoped that Escobedo and Harrigan could work out their problems without anyone getting hurt.

But regardless of all that, Longarm knew that the time had come for him to leave Las Hermanas del Fuego.

The five riders retraced the route Longarm had taken when he came to the ranch, following the valley past the towering twin volcanoes. As he rode along, Longarm studied the ridge that divided Don Manuel's land from that of Gordo Harrigan. It was a rugged, spiny barrier, split in a few places by high passes. Longarm wondered if the rangeland on the other side of the ridge was as good as that belonging to Don Manuel Escobedo.

Esteban was the taciturn sort, but Longarm decided to indulge his curiosity anyway. "Tell me about the fella who

71

owns the ranch on the other side of that ridge," he suggested. "The one they call El Gordo."

Esteban sent a quick, sharp glance in Longarm's direction. "What do you know of El Gordo?"

"Not a whole hell of a lot, old son. That's why I'm asking."

Esteban gave a snort of disgust. "Do not honor the pig by giving him a Spanish name. He is an Irishman, the bastard son of an Indian woman and a soldier of fortune who fought for Santa Anna during the last war with your country."

"Is that so? Why does he call himself El Gordo?"

"He says he is a Mexican now," Esteban replied with a shrug. "He must feel that he needs a Mexican name. The pig."

"Sounds like you don't much like him," Longarm said dryly.

Esteban leaned over in the saddle and spat on the ground. "He would like to drive Don Manuel out of the valley and claim this ranch for his own. He is a thief at heart. I think he must have been a thief and a smuggler before he came here. He is not a man who would have worked at an honest profession."

"You say he's trying to drive you out, but what's he actually done?" Longarm asked. He knew that this was none of his business, that he was on his way back to Texas and would probably never return here despite what he had said to Dulcey, but still his nagging curiosity made him voice the question.

"We have found dead cattle," Esteban said grimly. "In the old days, when the Yaquis still roamed these mountains, they would kill a steer from time to time for meat. Now the Yaquis have gone west, and the cattle we find dead have been shot and left to rot." The vaquero's voice trembled a little with the depth of emotion he was feeling. A true cowman hated to see beeves go to waste, whether north or south of the border, and at this moment, Longarm knew that Esteban was a true cowman.

"That is not all," Esteban went on. "One of our pastures was burned. Streams have been fouled. And three of our caballeros have been shot from ambush. Two of them died, and the third man will never walk or ride a horse again. The bullet came from nowhere and broke his back. He wishes he had been killed, too."

Longarm nodded slowly. What Esteban was describing sounded like one outfit on the prod for another, sure enough. "Has any of this been reported to the authorities?" he asked.

"The authorities?" Esteban repeated, then gave a scornful laugh. "Do you know anything about the *Rurales*?"

As a matter of fact, Longarm knew more than he wanted to about the Mexican federal police force responsible for patrolling these far-flung northern states. During his forays across the border, he had clashed with them more than once, usually to his regret. The *Rurales* were notorious for their corruption, but even worse than that, they were one of the most inefficient bunches of what passed for lawmen that Longarm had ever run across. There were a few good men scattered through their ranks, Longarm had discovered, but overall the group wasn't worth a bucketful of warm spit.

"Sorry I asked," he muttered to Esteban. "I know better."

The vaquero nodded. He tapped the butt of the pistol holstered at his waist. "This is the only real law here. And one day soon, I hope, we will teach Gordo Harrigan the folly of his greed."

Longarm rode along in silent discouragement for a while after that. Don Manuel Escobedo was an odd duck, but Longarm had liked him anyway. And Diablito and Esteban were good men, he had no doubt of that. Throw some innocents like Dulcey and Pablo and the elderly servant couple into the mix, and Longarm hated to think about a range war breaking out here in the valley. If it came down to open warfare between Don Manuel and Harrigan, that pretty little stream might run red with

73

blood. There was Don Manuel's sister Theresa to think of, too . . .

Maybe when he got back to Denver, he would ask Billy Vail to get in touch with the Justice Department and see if word could be passed to the Mexican government about the trouble brewing here in Chihuahua. It might not accomplish a thing, but at least Longarm would feel like he had tried to do something to help.

The green valley petered out, and the trail turned in a more northerly direction. With every mile, vegetation grew more sparse. Longarm had been unconscious during most of the trip from the border to the ranch, so he was seeing it with fresh eyes. The trouble with that was that there wasn't much to see except flat brown ground dotted with greasewood, sage, and mesquites. Longarm hipped around in the saddle and peered back toward the mountains. They loomed up, seemingly close enough to touch, and from the perspective of the desert heat, they looked cool and inviting.

Turned around as he was, Longarm didn't see exactly what happened. But he heard a dull thud, heard a man grunt in pain, a horse whinny in startled fear. Close beside Longarm, Esteban yelled a curse. Somewhere in there, Longarm thought he had heard the flat, distant report of a gun.

He twisted in the saddle and hauled back on the reins. A few yards away, one of the vaqueros toppled out of the saddle, a bloodstain blooming on his shirtfront where a bullet had hit him.

Something whined past Longarm's ear, sounding like a giant, angry insect. He knew the sound of a bullet all too well. He wasn't sure where the shots were coming from, but he knew that sitting still would just make him a better target. He jammed his boot heels into the flanks of the dun and yelled to the horse. The dun leaped into a gallop, whirling to the side as Longarm jerked on the reins.

Esteban and the other men were moving, too. Esteban shouted, *"El arroyo!"* Then he waved to the right. He

74

knew the terrain around here better than Longarm did, so Longarm figured it would be best to follow. He fell in behind Esteban and the others.

Another slug whipped past him, singing its deadly song. A few yards ahead, another of the riders cried out and flung his hands high in the air. He tumbled out of the saddle and slammed to the ground, as limp as a rag doll. Longarm knew he was dead.

The lineback dun might not look like much, but the rangy animal was built for speed. In a matter of moments, Longarm pulled up even with Esteban. "Where are they?" he shouted over the pounding of hooves.

"Ahead of us somewhere," Esteban shouted back. "But there is an arroyo over there. If we can reach it before they cut us off, we can give a good account of ourselves!"

Longarm looked to the left, saw dust boiling in the air. After the first few volleys had emptied a couple of saddles, the bushwhackers had taken to their own horses and were racing now to prevent Longarm and his two companions from reaching shelter. It was hard to tell just from the amount of dust, but Longarm estimated at least half a dozen horses were kicking up that swirling cloud. That meant odds of two to one—if not worse.

Still, he and Esteban and the other man were all armed with revolvers, and the horses of the two dead vaqueros carried rifles as well. With adequate cover, they could put up a good fight, as Esteban said. But the bushwhackers were still angling toward them, trying to cut them off from the arroyo.

Esteban's body jerked, but he managed to stay in the saddle, hunched over the neck of his horse. The animal started to slow, but Esteban spurred it on. The arroyo was closer now, no more than fifty yards away. They were going to make it, Longarm thought.

Then the other vaquero's horse went down as a stray bullet ripped out its throat. The rider sailed over the horse's head and crashed into the sandy ground, his momentum carrying him in a roll across some prickly pear

75

cactus. When he came to a stop, the angle of his head and the fact that he wasn't even reacting to the scores of cactus spines that had lanced into him told Longarm that he was dead, his neck broken in the fall.

That meant he and Esteban were the only ones left, Longarm thought grimly, and Esteban had been hit. Still, it wasn't in either man to give up, so they galloped on toward the great slash in the ground formed by the arroyo.

They reached it well ahead of the killers. The riderless horses had followed Longarm and Esteban, empty stirrups flapping wildly. All five of the animals slid down the steep bank into the arroyo. Longarm was out of the saddle as soon as the dun's hooves touched the sandy bottom, and he leaped over to one of the other horses to drag a dead man's Winchester out of its saddle sheath.

Esteban half fell as he dismounted. He swayed but stayed on his feet. His left arm was pressed across his midsection. Longarm could see blood welling past that arm. Esteban was gut-shot.

That was a death sentence, more than likely, but for now, Esteban was still alive, and he was mad. He ripped his own rifle from its sheath and started trying to climb the bank. Longarm ran over to him, steadied him with a hand on his arm. Esteban glanced at him, and Longarm grinned.

"Let's give those bastards a hot lead howdy," Longarm said.

Esteban nodded grimly. The two men struggled to the top of the bank and knelt there. Esteban took his arm away from his belly so that he could prop both elbows on the ground to brace himself. His shirt and jacket were sodden with blood. His face was pale but determined.

Longarm settled down beside Esteban and peered over the sights of the Winchester in his hands. The bushwhackers were close enough so that he could see them, dark figures at the base of the wind-whipped dust cloud. Longarm and Esteban both started firing as fast as they could lever fresh rounds into the chambers of the rifles.

With angry shouts, the attackers peeled off, vanishing into the dust. Longarm stopped shooting. "They figured on wiping us out without much trouble," he said. "They didn't like it when they found out we've got fangs."

Esteban didn't make any reply, and when Longarm glanced over at the vaquero, he thought for an instant that he was dead. But then his eyes flickered open, and he turned his head to look at Longarm.

"Vamanos," Esteban said hoarsely. "Get out of here, Senor Custis."

Longarm shook his head. "I don't reckon there's anywhere to go."

Esteban reached over with a blood-smeared hand and tightly gripped Longarm's arm. "Follow . . . the arroyo!" he gasped, pointing with the barrel of the rifle he held in his other hand. "It runs . . . back to the edge of the mountains."

"Maybe so, but those fellas won't let me get there, old son. They'll be rushing us again in a minute or two, I'd wager."

"Yes, they will come . . . and I will slow them down. If you go now, you will have a chance!"

Longarm glanced along the narrow, twisting arroyo. "That'd mean leaving you here," he said.

"The time left to me . . . is numbered in minutes, my friend." Esteban gave a hollow chuckle. "I can think of no better way to spend it . . . than killing some of those murderers."

Longarm's jaw tightened. He knew that Esteban was right about one thing: the vaquero didn't have long to live. But he might be able to hold off the bushwhackers long enough to at least give Longarm a head start. The chances of him getting away were still mighty slim, but any chance was better than none.

"Leave that rifle for me," Esteban went on, "and get another from one of the horses. Take the dun. When you have to choose . . . follow the water."

Longarm wasn't sure what Esteban meant by that; this

77

arroyo was dry as a bone. But maybe it wasn't when it got closer to the mountains. He felt himself nodding and knew he had reached a decision.

"Muchas gracias, mi amigo," he murmured.

Esteban's fingers tightened on his arm again. "Tell Diablito—" A spasm of pain choked off the words. Esteban gasped, then forced himself to say, "Go! Now!"

Longarm nodded. *"Vaya con Dios."* He left the Winchester within easy reach of Esteban and slid down the bank.

The dun was still close by, as were the other horses. Longarm grabbed the dun's reins and snagged one of the other rifles. As he did so, gunshots began to pop again out on the plain. Esteban answered them, firing smoothly and steadily.

Longarm started along the arroyo, the sand of the bottom pulling at his boots and slowing him down. He led the dun. It took only a minute to reach the first bend in the dry gully. Longarm paused and glanced back at Esteban, kneeling there on the lip of the arroyo, firing at the attackers as blood formed a pool underneath him and began to trickle down the bank. The crimson stream disappeared, soaking quickly into the thirsty ground.

"Vaya con Dios," Longarm whispered again, and then he was gone, heading along the arroyo toward the mountains as fast as he could move.

Chapter 8

The shooting continued for several minutes after Longarm left Esteban. When it came to a halt, he figured that the vaquero was dead.

The bushwhackers must have made the same mistake, because suddenly there was a flurry of shots, the reports spitting out quick and vicious in the hot air. Most of the shots came from pistols this time. A savage grin tugged at the corners of Longarm's mouth. In his mind's eye, he could see those bushwhackers sneaking up to the arroyo to check on their victims. They were probably surprised as hell when a bloody apparition reared up and greeted them with a storm of lead.

Longarm hoped that Esteban was the last thing a few of the buzzards had seen as he blasted them straight into *El Infierno*.

Longarm kept moving as the shooting died away. This time it wouldn't start again, he knew. Esteban had been finished off.

When the bushwhackers went down into the arroyo, it wouldn't take them long to see that one of their intended victims had gotten away. The sand on the floor of the gully held tracks. If Longarm had been in charge of the gang of killers, he would have sent some of them along the bottom of the gully while ordering the others to return to their horses and follow the arroyo up on the flatland. Longarm had gone only a few hundred yards since leaving Esteban. The gunmen would catch up to him in minutes.

Unless he did something to throw them off the scent. His eyes lit up with hope as he saw that the arroyo forked up ahead. He hesitated, uncertain which branch of the gully to take. They were both about the same size, and neither seemed more traveled than the other.

Longarm's eyes narrowed as he studied the banks. In the gully to the left, the banks were more deeply scoured than in the one on the right. He knew how such things worked in desert country: these arroyos stayed dry for months on end, and then a cloudburst in the mountains sent walls of water flooding down them. That fast-moving water carved marks on the sandstone walls of the arroyos, and the fact that the one on the left bore more pronounced markings told Longarm that it was the main channel in times of flooding.

That meant it followed a more direct path to the mountains, instead of meandering around in the desert. *Follow the water,* Esteban had said. Now Longarm understood.

He slapped the dun on the rump and sent it galloping down the right-hand branch of the arroyo. When the startled horse had vanished around a bend, Longarm started up the left-hand branch on foot, staying as close as he could to the bank where the ground was harder and his footprints would be less noticeable.

He hated to lose the dun, but confusing his pursuers was his only chance to get away. He moved quickly with the Winchester held slanted across his chest. His hope was that the killers would follow the horse's tracks for a few more minutes anyway. If they were on horseback, he now had the other branch of the gully between him and them, and that would slow them down, too.

As he moved along the arroyo in a trot, he became aware that the ground had acquired a gradual slope. As always, the desert was not as flat as it appeared to the casual observer. Longarm felt confident now that this path would lead him to the mountains. Once he was there, giving his pursuers the slip would be even easier.

Longarm began to think that maybe he would come out of this mess alive after all.

He had been moving along the arroyo for a quarter of an hour when he heard voices behind him. They were faint but definitely there. Longarm grimaced. Either the bushwhackers had found his tracks, or they had split up to follow both branches of the arroyo. Since he didn't know how many of them there were, he couldn't be sure what they were capable of.

He kept up his trot, trying to listen behind him as he did so. The voices grew louder. They had to be on horseback, he figured. And they were closing in on him.

Well, that tore it. He wasn't going to get away without a fight. In that case, it made more sense for him to choose the time and place of the gunplay.

He broke into a run as he entered a long, straight stretch. There were no rocks or crevices anywhere along either bank that he could use for cover. If the gunmen caught up with him now, they would have him in their sights like he was a duck in a shooting gallery. He had to reach the next bend before they emerged behind him.

Longarm thought about climbing out of the arroyo, but the walls were too sheer along here. He was trapped, just as he had been at the bottom of Santa Elena Canyon. Instead of a raging river, there were only sand and pebbles on the bottom of this gully, but he was still carried ahead just as he had been by the Rio Grande.

He heard hoofbeats behind him. They were muffled by the sand, so he couldn't tell how close they were. He forged on, his face covered with sweat, his eyes fixed on the bend ahead of him. It was perhaps twenty yards away now.

Suddenly, someone whooped triumphantly behind him. He twisted around and saw two horsebackers galloping around the bend he had passed several minutes earlier. They rode toward him, yelling and shooting.

Longarm dropped to one knee, brought the Winchester to his shoulder in a blur of motion, and sighted in the blink of an eye. The rifle cracked, and one of the over-eager bushwhackers went flying backward out of his saddle, flipping over once completely before he crashed to the ground.

That made the other one draw rein in a hurry. He had to be realizing right about now that if Longarm had no place to hide, neither did he. The rifle barked again as the gunman whirled his horse around. Longarm knew he had missed. He levered another shell into the Winchester's chamber and fired a third time. Another miss, but it was close enough that it sent the rider dusting for the shelter of the bend he had just passed.

Longarm was on his feet instantly, sprinting for cover himself. He darted around the next turn in the arroyo and stopped to press his back against the wall of the gully. His heart was pounding heavily. He had cut down the odds against him, but not enough. Those shots would bring the rest of the bushwhackers in a hurry.

He sleeved sweat off his face and looked the other direction along the arroyo. It branched again not far off, he saw. It was like a spiderweb, some of the strands leading to the mountains while others spun off into dead ends.

With another man down, the killers would be more cautious now. Even if that bought Longarm only a few extra minutes, he intended to take advantage of them. He drew in a deep breath and started running again, silently cursing the soft sand that tugged at his boots.

Again he followed the watermarks in the walls of the arroyo, backtracking the freshets that had carved out these usually arid gashes in the landscape. He glanced up at the mountains. They looked close, but no closer than they had been before the ambush. Was he really getting nearer to them, he asked himself, or was he just fooling himself?

When some scrubby trees began appearing above him

on the banks of the gully, he knew that he really was approaching the foothills. He came to a place where part of the overhang had collapsed at some time in the past, bringing one of the trees down with it. The tree was dead now. Longarm considered hiding behind it to set up an ambush of his own, but he decided that the trunk and the branches didn't offer enough protection from bullets. Maybe the tree could serve another purpose, though.

He leaned the gun against the wall of the arroyo and grasped the trunk of the fallen tree. With a grunt of effort, he lifted it and swung it around so that it blocked most of the narrow gully. Some dried brush had caught in the branches, probably from the last time there had been a flash flood. Longarm pulled the brush free and stacked it at the end of the tree to fill in the remaining gap. Then he took a lucifer from his pocket, flicked the match into life with an iron-hard thumbnail, and tossed the little flame into the brush.

The dry stuff went up like tinder. The fire caught hold in a hurry and spread to the branches of the tree. It began to pop and crackle and smoke curled into the air. Longarm backed away, grabbed up the rifle, and turned to run again. He cast a glance over his shoulder a moment later and saw that the tree was burning all along its length now. He grinned.

That would slow down the pursuit for quite a while, he thought. The horses wouldn't want to get near the fire, and the flames would keep the gunmen from pulling the barrier out of the way. They might be able to lasso it and haul it aside that way, but that wouldn't be easy. They could wind up not accomplishing anything except burning their ropes in two.

Longarm pounded on as smoke rose behind him from the blazing tree. The arroyo forked several more times as it entered the foothills. It seemed like Longarm had been running forever. He stopped occasionally but never rested more than a few seconds.

As soon as he came to a place where he could climb

the bank, he scrambled out of the arroyo. If he had still been down on the plain, anyone on horseback would have stood a good chance of spotting him. The terrain was more rugged here, however. Longarm trotted along, never skylighting himself, following the folds of land that rolled up to the Sierra de Santa Elena.

The smoke was gone now, the fire burned out. But it had served its purpose, Longarm hoped. He stopped and looked for dust or another sign of pursuit, but didn't see any.

Holding the rifle at his side in his right hand, Longarm wiped the back of his left across his mouth. It was starting to look as if he had given the bushwhackers the slip.

The sudden whinny of a horse made him whirl around and bring up the Winchester. He stopped his finger just short of pulling the trigger.

The lineback dun he had been riding earlier stood about a hundred yards away at the edge of a grove of cedar. The saddle was still on the horse's back. The dun must have climbed out of the arroyo at some point, just as Longarm had, and wandered up here.

A feeling of relief so tangible it almost hurt went through Longarm. He started walking slowly toward the horse, talking softly as he approached so that the dun wouldn't spook. If the horse didn't turn and bolt, Longarm knew that his chances of getting away from the killers would improve tremendously.

The dun was a little skittish, and a couple of times Longarm's heart leaped into his throat when he thought the horse was going to gallop off. In the end, though, its curiosity won out over its nervousness. The dun allowed Longarm to walk up to it and take hold of the reins.

Longarm scratched the dun's nose and told it what a wonderful horse it was. He took hold of the saddle horn, got his foot in the stirrup, and swung up. There was no saddle sheath for the Winchester, so he had to carry the rifle across the saddle in front of him as he turned the dun toward the high, snowcapped peaks.

He wanted to put both distance and height between himself and his pursuers—if, in fact, the bushwhackers were still on his trail. Longarm knew how lucky he had been to escape so far. He didn't want to blunder now. The high ground would give him a slight advantage, or at least help even the odds, if the killers caught up to him.

He rode until after midday before stopping to rest the dun. The horse was strong and didn't seem to mind carrying him. The breed that never dies, Diablito had called it, and the big *segundo* was right.

Longarm wondered what it was Esteban had wanted him to tell Diablito. He would never know, but he could guess that it had been some expression of friendship and respect. He would tell that to Diablito when he got back to Las Hermanas del Fuego.

Longarm wasn't sure when he had reached the decision to return to the ranch. He didn't know if it had been a conscious decision. But that was where he was going, he was certain of that. Don Manuel had to be told what had happened.

For the first time, Longarm gave some thought to the identity of the killers. Were they some of Gordo Harrigan's men? That seemed to be the most likely explanation. Esteban had said that some of the vaqueros who rode for the Escobedo brand had been bushwhacked in the past by Harrigan's men. It was reasonable to assume that the attack today was another in that series of murderous outrages.

Being shot at didn't sit well with Longarm. He didn't cotton to such things at all. Maybe he would postpone his return to Texas for a little while after all and try to help Don Manuel straighten out this mess with Harrigan. Billy Vail wouldn't like that when—and if—he heard about it, but by that time the whole thing would be over, a fate accomplished or whatever that saying was.

Longarm mounted up again and rode higher into the wilderness of volcanic peaks. He realized he was following the ridge that ran between Don Manuel's ranch and

Harrigan's spread. He reined in on a high ledge and studied the country that fell away beneath him. It was a jumble of rock spires and talus slopes, with occasional pockets of green tucked away in the stony barrens.

Movement across one of those small patches of vegetation caught his eye. Longarm leaned forward in the saddle, and his gaze narrowed as he tried to make out what he was seeing. The meadow was probably a thousand yards below him, but in the clear mountain air, his keen eyes picked out the shapes of several riders.

They had to be the bushwhackers, Longarm thought with a stir of excitement. Nobody else had any reason to be up here in the middle of nowhere. They had given up the chase, and now they were on their way back to wherever they had come from. That was the only explanation that made any sense.

Longarm glanced to his right. If the riders kept climbing steadily over the next mile, they would reach one of the passes that led to Harrigan's range. If they crossed over, that would be confirmation enough for Longarm that they worked for the expatriate Irishman.

A grin touched Longarm's tanned face. If he was careful, he could follow them, maybe get the drop on them.

It was fitting, he thought, that the hunters would become the hunted.

He hitched the dun into motion and let the sure-footed cayuse pick its way along the faint mountain trail. As he swayed slightly in the saddle, he kept an eye on the riders far below. Sometimes they vanished from his sight for several minutes at a time, but they always reappeared as the trail they were following swung back around into Longarm's view.

The bushwhackers climbed to the pass, just as Longarm expected. They were closer to being on the same level as him now, so he hung back, watching them from a quarter of a mile away behind a screen of juniper. Not much grew this high up, so Longarm took advantage of whatever cover he could find, just in case one of the killers looked behind him.

None of them seemed to be paying much attention to their back trail, though. They had given up on finding Longarm, and they sure as hell wouldn't be expecting him to be tracking them. As the last of the bunch disappeared through the pass, Longarm patted the dun's shoulder and said, "There they go, old son, back where they came from, I reckon."

He heeled the horse into motion. It was possible the bushwhackers might have left a rear guard at the pass, but Longarm didn't think it was very likely. Still, he approached cautiously, alert for any sign of trouble.

He reined in and swung down from the saddle before he reached the pass, then went forward on foot, his hands taut on the Winchester. Ducking from one boulder to another, he slipped into the rock-littered cut in the ridge and took a look around. After a couple of minutes, he decided there were no sentries lurking around the pass.

Moving up so that he could see down the far side of the ridge, Longarm knelt beside a large rock and scanned the rugged terrain until he spotted the riders. They were still moving, and he was close enough to them now so that he could count them. Eight men were left. Considering that he had killed one man and Esteban probably had downed two or three of them, that meant the gang had numbered around a dozen starting out. They'd had better than two to one odds on their side when they set out to bushwhack Longarm and his companions. They had wanted to make sure of their killings.

But in that, they had failed. Longarm was still alive. He hurried back to the dun, mounted up, and rode after the gunmen.

If they had been alert, he might not have been able to follow them as they worked their way along the ridge toward the two towering, dormant volcanoes. But they were obviously disgusted with themselves for allowing one of their prey to get away, and they never looked back.

Still, Longarm didn't crowd them too closely. The clinking sound of a horseshoe hitting a rock could carry a long way in this clear, thin air.

For the first time, Longarm got a good look at the range claimed by Gordo Harrigan. The valley on this side of the ridge was neither as broad nor as fertile as the one where Don Manuel's ranch was located. Nor did it have a creek running through it. No doubt there were some water holes here and there, maybe a few spring-fed trickles, but water would be scarcer over here. As a result, the grass was not as widespread or as lush. There was enough graze, Longarm estimated, for a herd about half the size of the one Don Manuel Escobedo ran. No wonder Harrigan was jealous.

A few minutes later, Longarm reined in and frowned in surprise as the killers he was following changed direction. No longer did they work their way down toward the floor of the valley. Instead, they started to climb again. They were practically underneath the nearer of the two Sisters of Fire by now. Longarm watched as they followed a zig-zag trail up the shoulder of the mountain and finally disappeared around a bend.

It wouldn't do for him to follow them out in the open, he decided. The mountainside was too open for that; even careless men would spot him. He would have to get above them again.

He stared at the slope above the trail the killers had followed and saw a faint line sketched across the mountain. "Hope you're part goat, old son," he said as he patted the dun again. "You'll need to be to follow that upper trail."

Longarm hitched the horse into a walk. They climbed the slope, which was dotted here and there with scrawny trees and bushes. When they reached the beginning of the upper trail, Longarm saw that it was as narrow and twisting as he had feared. The dun took to it without hesitation, however. He hoped like hell the horse knew what it was doing.

It wasn't long before they had climbed to dizzying heights. The mountainside fell away steeply on Longarm's right and rose just as steeply on his left. His left stirrup brushed rock wall while his right hung over hundreds of feet of empty air.

Around and around the trail curved, hugging the mountain. Again, Longarm found himself well past the point of no return. There was no way the horse could back down the trail, and Longarm couldn't dismount. "Easy, hoss, easy," he breathed to the dun. "Just take it slow and steady."

Down below, the trees thickened. Longarm gazed down at the tops of pines and cedars. That was where the lower trail led, he realized. The bushwhackers had been heading for this park-like area that *El Senor Dios* had dropped on the side of the barren mountain for some reason known only to him.

Longarm breathed shallowly as the trail he was on dipped and turned. His gizzard was trying to climb up his throat. The dun turned another corner . . . and then suddenly the trail widened out. It formed a ledge about eight feet wide—which at this moment looked almost as broad to Longarm as the Mississippi River.

He angled the horse over next to the cliff and dismounted. His knees trembled a little, but only for a moment. That ride up the mountain had been as harrowing an experience as he had gone through since the crazy ride down the Rio Grande, and he wasn't anxious to repeat it anytime soon.

He cast a glance up at the sky and saw to his surprise that the sun was low in the west, not far from slipping behind the mountains to bring on nightfall. He had tracked the bushwhackers all day without really being aware of the passage of time.

A mixture of two familiar smells drifted to his nose: woodsmoke and roasting meat. The bushwhackers had made camp somewhere below him. He looked for smoke and didn't see any. They were keeping their fire small, and they probably had erected a screen of slender branches above it to disperse the smoke. Longarm hunkered at the edge of the place where he had stopped and stared down at the woods below.

After a few minutes, he thought he had the fire spotted. As the sun dipped below the peaks and dusk came on with its usual sudden rush, he was sure of it. He could see the flames from up here, but they would be invisible from lower down on the mountain. The only ones who knew where the killers were camped were him and a few buzzards, hawks, and mountain goats.

He wanted to get down there, but he didn't see any possible way to do it. Before it became completely dark, he explored along the trail. It grew narrow again, but about fifty yards past where he'd left the dun, Longarm found a chimney hewn into the rock by natural forces. It was narrow enough so that he could brace himself in it and work his way down.

Longarm frowned in thought as he rasped a thumbnail along his jaw. Getting down there would be fairly easy, but getting up again would be harder and take longer. If he ran into trouble, he couldn't retreat in a hurry. And he was outnumbered eight to one, he reminded himself.

But if he could get close enough to eavesdrop on the bushwhackers, he might be able to find out why they had tried to wipe out the party of riders heading for the border. He had thought at first they were Harrigan's men, but if that were the case, why hadn't they just gone back to Harrigan's hacienda? Why make such an isolated camp on the side of a mountain?

Longarm made up his mind. He returned to the dun long enough to tie a fist-sized rock to the reins and leave them dangling so that the horse wouldn't wander off. He left the Winchester lying there, too, since he knew he couldn't handle it in the chimney.

He went back to the cleft in the rock and sat down on the edge. Bracing his boots against the far side, he slid off the brink and straightened his legs. His back was pressed hard enough against the near side to keep him from falling. Slowly, he began working his way down.

By the time he got to the bottom, the muscles in his legs ached like blazes from the strain and his back was scraped painfully in several places. When he dropped the last foot or so and was back on solid ground, relief washed through him.

He was still higher than the place where the bush-whackers had made their camp, but only by about forty feet. He had fixed the location in his mind and was glad of that, because he could no longer see the fire. He slipped closer, moving with the catlike stealth that often took enemies by surprise because they didn't expect such a big man to be able to get around so smoothly and silently.

Voices came to his ears, and the smell of food was stronger. Longarm's stomach clenched, reminding him that he hadn't eaten since that morning on the trail. Some of the food Don Manuel had sent with him was still in the saddlebags, but Longarm had been too occupied with other things to eat any of it.

He ghosted through some brush and then knelt motion-less, able at last to see through a screen of branches to the campfire. He saw men moving around it, eating and talking quietly and passing a bottle back and forth. The bushwhackers were speaking Spanish. Most of the accents Longarm heard were Mexican, but he was convinced there were a few gringos in the group, too.

The sound of hoofbeats in the night made Longarm stiffen, and it provoked a reaction from the men around the fire, too. They came to their feet. Guns whispered from leather. Shells were jacked into rifle chambers with the metallic sound of levers being worked. The hoofbeats stopped as the rider approaching the camp reined to a halt.

"Hello, the camp."

The voice belonged to an American, though the words were Spanish. Longarm's jaw tightened. Something about the sound of the voice was familiar, but he couldn't place it.

91

One of the gunmen called, "Come on in." A moment later, a large shape loomed up at the edge of the small circle of light cast by the fire. The figure split in two, turned into a man climbing down off a horse. Holding the reins, he came a step closer to the flames, and the flickering light illuminated a face Longarm had seen before.

Not in person, though. The only time Longarm had seen this man before, his face had been in shadow and his body silhouetted against a star-dappled night sky on the other side of the border. Longarm knew him anyway.

Victoria Canfield was a good artist. That painting of hers Longarm had looked at back in Lajitas had captured Peter Braddock perfectly.

Chapter 9

"Hello, boys," Braddock said. "How did it go?"

The sombrero-wearing pistolero who had invited Braddock into the camp spat in the fire and said, "All dead except one."

Braddock frowned. "Which one?"

"The tall man, the one who looked like a gringo."

"Son of a bitch!" Braddock burst out. "El Gordo's not going to be happy to hear that."

Out in the brush where he crouched watching and listening, Longarm's brain was spinning in confusion. Not only was it shocking enough to see Peter Braddock here below the border acting like one of the gang, but obviously Braddock had some connection with Gordo Harrigan, too. What the hell was going on here?

"There was nothing we could do," the Mexican protested. "That big one, he is a slippery bastard."

Braddock hunkered on his heels next to the fire and intercepted the bottle of rotgut as it went around the circle of killers. He tipped it up and let some of the fiery stuff gurgle into his mouth. When he had lowered the bottle and passed it on, he said, "I know. I thought I'd killed him more than a week ago. Drop a man off a cliff into the rapids of the Rio Grande and the least he could do is have the common courtesy to go ahead and die."

Longarm's jaw was tight as he listened. He felt anger welling up inside him. He wanted to march into the camp and knock that arrogant smirk right off Braddock's face. But doing that wouldn't accomplish anything except to get himself killed. With an effort, he reined in his temper.

One of the other gunmen asked, "You think this big gringo is after you, Senor Braddock?" The tone of deference in the man's voice told Longarm that Braddock was an important fella in this neck of the woods.

"I don't know why he's down here," Braddock replied. "Like I said, I figured he was dead. If he's got any sense, he lit out for the border when he got away from you boys."

The frown on Longarm's face deepened. Braddock hadn't referred to him as a deputy U.S. marshal, and Longarm couldn't tell if the others knew he was an American lawman or not. But if Braddock had told them other things about Longarm, why would he have withheld that particular bit of information?

And how had Braddock found out that Longarm was going to be riding toward the border with some of Don Manuel's vaqueros today? How had he even found out that Longarm was still alive?

Too damned many questions, Longarm thought. And it didn't look like he was going to get any answers anytime soon, because the men around the fire started telling bawdy stories and passing around another bottle of tequila. Before long, they would all be dozing off into a drunken slumber.

Even so, there were too many of them for Longarm to risk making an attempt to capture them. It made more sense, he decided, to try to find Gordo Harrigan's ranch and do a little scouting around there. Clearly, there was a connection between Harrigan and the gang of bushwhackers, even though they hadn't gone to his hacienda. Right now, Longarm needed information more than anything else.

He didn't give any thought to the fact that he was operating below the border, where he had no jurisdiction. He had been shot at and his companions had been killed, and that was more than enough to make Longarm stop worrying about any technicalities. Besides, Peter Braddock was a fugitive from American justice, and his unexpected appearance gave Longarm the excuse he needed to stay here and try to sort out this mess.

He backed away from the camp, moving silently through the brush and across the rocks until he got back to the chimney that led up to the ledge high above. As he expected, going up was a lot more difficult than coming down, and a lot slower, too. Longarm wedged himself into the chimney and carefully worked his way toward the top. When he got there and rolled onto the ledge that formed the upper trail, he lay there for several minutes, unmoving except for the rapid rise and fall of his chest. His right leg ached fiercely, and he felt as weak as could be. He had pushed his body hard today, and now the time he had been laid up was taking its toll.

Gradually, some of his strength came back to him. He was able to get up and walk over to the dun. He gulped some water from the canteen that was looped over the saddle horn and ate a couple of tortillas he took out of the saddlebags. Feeling a little better, he led the horse over to the path that would take them back down the mountain. This time instead of mounting up, Longarm went ahead on foot, the dun's reins gripped tightly in his hand.

If the trip up had been bad in daylight, the trip down was worse at night. Longarm felt his way carefully along the trail, sliding his feet only a few inches at a time and keeping one hand on the rock wall beside him. Once, when he accidentally knocked a pebble off the path, it was a long, long time before he heard the faint clatter that marked its landing.

Descending took more than an hour. It seemed even

95

longer to Longarm. When he was finally on relatively level ground again, he swung up onto the dun and rode toward the center of the valley. He had no idea where Gordo Harrigan's hacienda was located, but he was sure he could find it by working his way across the valley. If there were any lights burning, that would make his job easier. Since Harrigan had no reason to suspect that anyone would be lurking around his ranch tonight, he wouldn't have taken the precaution of ordering the lamps put out.

Less than half an hour later, Longarm spotted what looked like a tiny yellow eye staring at him. He pointed the dun in that direction, and when he got closer, he could see several more spots of light. He kept the horse at a slow walk so the noise of hoofbeats wouldn't betray his approach. Within a few minutes he could discern in the starlight the buildings that made up Gordo Harrigan's hacienda.

The main house was adobe, smaller and less rambling than Don Manuel Escobedo's house, but set up along similar lines. The outbuildings were much the same, too, though even in the dark Longarm could tell they were more run-down. One small light glowed in the bunkhouse. The other lighted windows were in the main house.

Longarm made that his target. He dismounted in a small clump of trees and left the dun there with its reins tied to a bush. On foot, he slipped toward the hacienda. As he drew closer, he reached across his body and made sure that his Colt was loose in its holster. He intended to avoid trouble if at all possible, but sometimes a fella didn't get that choice.

Suddenly, the strains of guitar music drifted through the night from the bunkhouse, followed a moment later by a snatch of song. One of Harrigan's vaqueros sang a mournful tune. Longarm paused, lulled into a halt for a moment by the seductive sound. Then, with a little shake of his head he pressed on, forcing himself to ignore the plaintive melody.

He came to the eight-foot-tall, ten-inch-thick outer wall of the hacienda. Normally, it would not have been difficult for Longarm to leap up, grasp the top and pull himself over the wall. Tonight, in his weakened condition, it was more of a struggle, especially to do so quietly. He managed, though, and in a few minutes dropped to the ground in the outer courtyard. The place was laid out in a rectangle, with the house itself forming the rear wall of the enclosure. There would be another, smaller courtyard inside the house. Getting in there might prove to be impossible. For now Longarm would settle for slipping up on the lighted window he saw not far away.

He stayed low, crouching as he approached the house. He took off his hat as he reached the wall and pressed his back against the cool adobe. Breathing shallowly, he listened intently and waited for something to happen.

He didn't have to wait long. A burst of rapid Spanish came to his ears, the words tumbling out so fast Longarm had to strain to keep up. He didn't catch all of the conversation, which evidently was between two servants passing by inside the house, but he made out the words *El Gordo* and *Senorita Theresa*.

"He goes to her . . . tonight . . . will no longer tolerate . . . refusal . . ."

Longarm frowned as the voices faded away. From what Pablo had told him back at Las Hermanas del Fuego, it had sounded as if Theresa Escobedo was here at Harrigan's ranch of her own free will, living with Harrigan and bringing shame to her brother. But that wasn't the way the conversation he had just overheard made it sound. Of course, the sketchy nature of it made it difficult to obtain a perfectly clear understanding, but it sounded to Longarm like Theresa Escobedo was El Gordo's prisoner.

More questions and still no answers, he thought. But if Theresa was being held here against her will, he couldn't ignore that fact. He would have to try to help her.

If he could locate her, and that was a damned big question all by its lonesome. He sidled away from the window, straightened from his crouch, and began moving along the adobe wall.

When he reached the angle formed by the wall of the house and the outer wall, he climbed up again and found himself within reach of a wrought-iron railing that ran along a balcony on the house's second floor. Longarm stretched out, got a good hold on the railing with his right hand, and let himself swing out away from the wall. He got his left hand on the railing and pulled his weight up until he could hook a boot toe in the railing and take some of the strain off his arms. In seconds, he was over the railing and on the thick beams that made up the floor of the balcony.

From there he was able to climb up and balance on the rail while he got a grip on the tiles that made up the roof of the hacienda. With a grunt of effort he hauled himself onto the roof and sprawled out on it.

The roof had a gradual slope. Longarm had no trouble climbing to its peak and then letting himself down the far side. When he reached the edge, he was looking down into the inner courtyard that he had known had to be there. Again, it was smaller and not as well kept up as the one at Don Manuel's house. Longarm lay there on the roof for several minutes, catching his breath and listening.

When he heard a faint sound of sobbing, he knew he was on the right track. He crawled in the direction of the crying, and when he seemed to be right over it, he took off his hat and leaned down so that he could peer into the window below him.

Gauzy curtains of white lace hung over the windows, but they weren't enough to keep Longarm from being able to see into the room. It was a bedchamber lit by a single candle that sat on a small dressing table. The table, a chair, and a narrow bed were the only items of furniture in the room. There was no rug on the floor. Decoratively shaped iron bars were set in the window frame, adding to the impression that this room was little more than a jail cell. More comfortable than most *juzgados*, to be sure, but still a cell.

The young woman who sat on the bed, sobbing into her hands as she pressed them to her face, looked like a prisoner, too. She wore a white blouse and a simple skirt. Dark, straight hair hung around her shoulders. Longarm couldn't see her face because of her hands, but he was willing to bet that she was lovely. Her hair was thick and as glossy as a raven's wing, and the olive skin of her bare shoulders was smooth and inviting.

Longarm was almost certain he was looking at Theresa Escobedo.

The senorita was definitely upset about something, and Longarm had a pretty good idea what it was. The conversation he had overheard indicated that El Gordo was coming here to Theresa's room tonight to force himself on her.

Longarm studied the bars in the window. They looked solid, too solid to move. He might have been able to yank them loose from the adobe if he could have tied a rope to them and used his horse to pull on them, but that wasn't going to be possible. Given a knife and enough time, he could have loosened them that way, too. But that wasn't going to happen, either. There was also the problem of the room being on the second floor.

As far as Longarm could see, there was no way to get Theresa out of that room other than the door, which was thick and heavy and no doubt barred on the outside, maybe even guarded. He considered calling out softly to Theresa to let her know that he was out here and that he would try to help her, but until he came up with some plan, informing her of his presence wouldn't accomplish anything except perhaps to get her hopes up.

Before Longarm could do or say anything, heavy footsteps sounded in the corridor on the other side of the door. He heard the rattle of a padlock. So the door wasn't barred after all, just locked securely. He made a mental note of that.

Theresa looked up in fear at the sound of someone at the door. Longarm saw that his guess had been correct. Even streaked with tears and strained with fear, the face of the senorita was lovely, indeed. Her dark eyes were wide with apprehension. She shrank back on the bed as the door swung open.

The man who stood framed in the doorway was stocky but not really fat. Longarm knew he had to be Gordo Harrigan. He dressed like a vaquero but had pale skin, long red hair, and a red beard. He stepped into the room and lifted a hand toward the woman on the bed, not in a threatening way but more like an entreaty.

"Theresa," he said. "My darling."

Well, Longarm thought, at least he had confirmation now that the woman was Theresa Escobedo.

Theresa shrank back even more. "L-Leave me alone," she said.

"Have I harmed you in any way?" Harrigan demanded. "For weeks now, I have treated you as an honored guest in my house."

"An honored guest?" Theresa repeated, and for the first time, Longarm saw a spark of anger in her eyes. "I am your prisoner! You stole me from my home and made my brother believe I came with you willingly!"

Harrigan's back stiffened, and some anger of his own tightened his jaw. "The arrangements were all made properly," he said. "You were to be my bride. I had every right to bring you here."

"No! Manuel called off the wedding when he found out you had been stealing his cattle and killing his men. You know this!"

Harrigan took a step toward her. "I am not a thief!" he roared. "Not anymore! I came here to be an honest rancher!"

Theresa just gave him a look of tearful scorn.

Harrigan began to pace back and forth, staying between Theresa and the open door so that she couldn't make a dash for freedom. He smacked his right fist into his left palm. "Your brother is a fool," he said. "If anyone is the thief here, it is him. He stole your affections away from me, after promising you to me as my bride."

"You must let me go," Theresa begged. "You know you cannot keep me here."

Harrigan smiled. "Oh, but I can."

"I will never love you," Theresa said in a half-whisper.

"I think you will." Harrigan stopped pacing and took a step toward her. "For weeks I've allowed you to turn me away, hoping that you would come to see how I feel about you. But my heart burns with desire for you, Theresa. I can't deny it any longer. You *will* come to love me. Once I've held you in my arms, you'll see—"

"No!" she screamed as he came toward her.

Longarm's hand started instinctively toward his gun. Hanging upside down like this made for a tricky shot, but he figured he could fire between the bars in the window and plug Harrigan.

But even with Harrigan wounded or dead, Theresa would still be trapped, and Longarm would still be in the middle of enemy territory. Maybe it would be better, he thought, if he could draw Harrigan away somehow, get him out of the room before he could force himself on Theresa.

Even as Longarm reached that decision, he was already moving. His hand shot out—not toward his gun—but to grasp one of the tiles that formed the roof. He shoved hard and sent the tile sliding off the edge. It fell and shattered with a loud crash in the courtyard.

"What the hell?" Harrigan cried out in the room below Longarm. "What was that?"

Others had heard the noise besides the master of the hacienda. Shouts and questions rose from elsewhere in the house as Longarm rolled back away from the edge of the roof. He lay there as the commotion grew louder. He heard the door of Theresa's room slam. After waiting a moment longer, he ventured another look and saw that Harrigan had left Theresa alone in the room. She sat on the bed, a look of relieved surprise on her lovely face.

Longarm pulled his head up and put his hat on. Probably, he had succeeded only in postponing Theresa's fate at Harrigan's hands, but at least he had bought a little time for her.

And he had bought trouble for himself as well. The hacienda was in an uproar now as servants hurried out into the courtyard to search for the source of the crash. A *mozo* carrying a lamp scuttled toward the fallen tile. Longarm knew that as soon as the servant saw the tile, he would look up to see where it had come from. Coming up on his hands and toes, Longarm scrambled for the peak of the roof.

He reached the top and rolled over onto the other side. Pausing to catch his breath, he heard Harrigan's angry voice down in the courtyard. "Spread out!" Harrigan bellowed to his men. "Somebody has to be up there! Find him!"

Longarm slid down the far side of the roof. His horse was tied in the trees a hundred yards away from the hacienda. He would need luck on his side to reach the dun and get away.

When he reached the edge of the roof, he dropped to the top of the outer wall. He almost lost his balance and fell but recovered at the last second. He ran lightly along the top of the wall as a gate slammed open somewhere nearby in the darkness.

Longarm knelt and let himself down off the wall, dangling for a second before letting go and dropping the last foot and a half. He landed running, but he had gone only a few steps before a shape loomed up in front of him. *"Patron!"* the man shouted as he grabbed at Longarm. "Over here!"

Longarm knocked the man's hands aside with a sweep of his left arm and threw his right fist in a short punch that jolted into the man's face. The vaquero stumbled back a step and fell. Longarm tried to leap past him, but the man grabbed his leg and hung on with a fierce tenacity.

Longarm kicked him in the face with his other foot, knocking him loose.

That slowed him down enough for a couple of other men to come running around the corner of the outer wall toward him. *"Alto!"* one of them shouted.

They didn't wait to see if Longarm was going to stop. Gun flashes split the darkness. Bullets thudded into the thick adobe wall near Longarm.

Longarm could have returned the fire, but he was more interested in getting away. He darted toward a corral, hoping that the men would stop shooting for fear of hitting the horses milling around nervously inside the pen. He ran around a corner of the enclosure and barreled into yet another vaquero running to see what all the uproar was about. Longarm grabbed the man's shirt and swung him around, slamming him against the thick poles that formed the corral. The man bounced off the fence and ran right into the punch that Longarm threw.

Men were shouting all around now. Longarm made it to a barn and slipped into the thick shadows next to the wall of the building. He stood still, hoping the pursuit would go around him.

The day had started so peacefully, he thought, but ever since he and Esteban and the other vaqueros from Don Manuel's ranch had run into that ambush, he had spent hours running and riding and shooting, clambering around the mountains and climbing on top of haciendas. He was just about worn down to the nub, and he wasn't sure how much longer he could keep this up. He needed a break from all these ruckuses.

It appeared he was going to get one, because with the soft scrape of a footstep beside him, a gun barrel was pressed to his head, and Gordo Harrigan's voice said, "Don't move, *cabrón,* or I'll blow your goddamned brains out."

Chapter 10

Longarm stood absolutely still. He had no doubt that Harrigan meant the threat. Here on this *rancho*, Harrigan was a law unto himself who would think nothing of shooting down an intruder.

"Step out where I can see you better," Harrigan went on. "Don't try anything funny, though. Take it slow and easy."

Longarm sidled away from the wall and out into the faint wash of starlight. Harrigan came with him, keeping up the pressure on the gun. Harrigan was confident to the point of carelessness, Longarm thought. He had gotten too close to the man he had taken prisoner. Longarm could have spun around and knocked the gun away before Harrigan could pull the trigger.

At least, on a good day, he could have. Longarm wasn't so sure about tonight. Not only that, but a lot of Harrigan's vaqueros were close by and a gunshot would have them all over him in a matter of seconds. For now, he had to admit that Harrigan had the drop on him.

Harrigan plucked Longarm's Colt from its holster and then finally moved back a step, out of easy reach. "Over here!" he shouted. "I've got him!"

To Longarm, he went on, "Who the hell are you, mister, and what are you doing here? You better have a good answer, or you'll be dead in about a minute."

The wheels of Longarm's brain were clicking over with incredible speed. He considered everything he knew about the situation, and out of all the options that flickered through his thoughts, only one seemed to hold out any hope of keeping him alive—for a while.

"You're lucky you're not the one who's dead, Harrigan," he drawled. "I could have gunned you down a dozen times while you were in that room with the girl—if I'd wanted to."

Harrigan made an angry, incoherent noise in his throat. "So you were up on the roof? I thought so! Why, damn it?"

"To prove to you that you need to hire me," Longarm said.

The cool response was so unexpected that Harrigan didn't say anything for a moment. While he stood there silently holding a gun on Longarm, several more men came hurrying up, also brandishing weapons. Longarm regarded them calmly, knowing that his life hung by a thread, but knowing as well that he couldn't afford to show any nerves right now.

"I asked you before—who the hell are you?" Harrigan grated.

"Name's Parker," Longarm said, falling back on an alias he used frequently, an alias that happened to be his real middle name.

"You're an American?"

"That's right. Things were a mite warm for me on the other side of the Rio, so when I heard there might be a shooting war brewing down here, I decided to take a *pasear* south of the border and see if one side or the other could use a good man."

The deception had sprung almost full-blown into Longarm's brain. At times in the past, he had masqueraded as a gunman for hire, and he knew that rumors of range wars circulated freely among that powdersmoke fraternity. In the group of bushwhackers he had spied on earlier tonight, there were several gringos, so it was obvious Harrigan had hired American gunmen in the past.

"Turn around," Harrigan said. Longarm did so, and when Harrigan was facing him, the man said, "What in blazes are you talking about?"

Longarm said, "You don't mind if I reach in my pocket and get a smoke, do you?"

Harrigan made a gargling noise, clearly frustrated by Longarm's brazen calm. "Go ahead," he said, "just take it slow."

Longarm fished out a cheroot and stuck it unlit in his mouth. Clenching his teeth on it, he said, "You're Gordo Harrigan, and word is that you're either at war or about to be with a fella named Escobedo who owns the ranch on the other side of that big ridge over yonder. I poked around and found out that much before I rode in here. I figure you're hiring guns, and I plan to be one of them."

Harrigan leaned closer, his face harsh in the starlight. "That don't explain what you were doing running around on the roof of my house."

Longarm shrugged and said, "Call it a demonstration. You need somebody siding your play who's better than what you've got now, Harrigan. If I was working for Escobedo, you'd be one dead hombre." Longarm glanced around at the other men. "Who's in charge of guarding the place, anyway? Hell, a ten-year-old girl could waltz right in here, pretty as you please."

One of the vaqueros let out a stream of curses in Spanish, and Longarm figured his sally had found its target.

"Take it easy, Tomas," Harrigan snapped. "Maybe Parker here has a point. I thought you posted guards just in case that bastard Escobedo tried something."

"*Si*, El Gordo," the man called Tomas said. "There are sentries all around—"

"Well, then, they must be either blind or stupid, because Parker got past 'em."

There was no substitute for blind luck, Longarm thought, because he hadn't seen any guards and obviously they hadn't seen him.

"Senor—" Tomas began.

"Never mind," Harrigan cut in. To Longarm, he asked, "You say your name is Parker?"

"That's right."

"I never heard of you."

"Maybe you haven't been in Texas for a while," Longarm replied, still cool and calm.

"Well, I reckon that's true. . . . You're a cold-nerved son of a bitch, aren't you?"

Longarm didn't say anything. The sort of man he was pretending to be wouldn't have in that situation.

"Tell you what, those rumors you heard have some truth to them," Harrigan went on. "I'm having trouble with Don Manuel Escobedo, plenty of trouble. Gun trouble. You want to be part of it?"

"That's why I'm here," Longarm said around the cheroot.

Harrigan jerked his bearded chin toward the vaquero called Tomas. "You've shown me a lot already tonight, Parker, but before I'll hire you, you've got to go through Tomas."

That brought a laugh from Tomas, and with a whisper of steel, he drew a long, heavy-bladed knife from a sheath at the small of his back. "I will wash away my failure, *patron*, in the blood of this gringo."

Even in this poor light, Longarm didn't let his face reveal what he was feeling inside. After all he had been through today, the idea of taking part in a knife fight with this lithe, wiry-muscled vaquero was almost more than he could comprehend. He thought about spinning around and trying to snatch his gun away from Harrigan, but such a move would only get him killed and the idea of pretending to be a hired gun was to buy time until he could get away from the ranch and maybe even rescue Theresa Escobedo.

107

He had no choice. He said, "Whatever you want, Harrigan. It don't make no never-mind to me."

"You have a knife?"

"Nope," Longarm said.

Harrigan drew his own blade and slapped the bone handle into Longarm's palm. "Now you do," Harrigan told him with a grin.

Longarm hefted the knife. It was a bowie, the blade long and thick, tapering down to a wickedly curved point that was sharp on both top and bottom. The balance was almost perfect. The knife was a beautiful weapon, Longarm thought.

"Let's get some light out here," Harrigan shouted.

In response to his order, two men came running with torches. They stood on either side of the irregular circle that Harrigan and his vaqueros formed around Longarm and Tomas. That ring of men was impenetrable, Longarm knew. The only way he would get out of here alive was to defend himself successfully against Tomas.

Tomas tossed his sombrero aside, so Longarm did the same with his Stetson. The vaquero began circling, holding his knife low in the manner of a man who was experienced at this deadly sport. Longarm kept a close eye on him in the flickering torchlight, watching for even the tiniest indication that Tomas was about to strike.

When the first move came, it was with the speed of a rattlesnake. A great cry went up from the spectators as Tomas darted forward and sent the tip of his blade spearing at Longarm's throat. Longarm darted out of the way, only to realize too late that Tomas's thrust was only a feint. The blade whipped down and to the side, and the tip raked along the muscles of Longarm's upper left arm. It burned like the fiery finger of *El Senor Dios* drawing a line down the big lawman's arm.

Longarm felt the wet heat of blood flowing out of the gash. He was able to force the pain out of his mind, but his arm still didn't want to respond to his commands.

Tomas laughed. "First blood to me!" he taunted. "I

could have killed you just as easily, gringo, but I did not want to end this too soon. You must suffer for your temerity!"

Longarm knew Tomas was trying to make him mad. "You sure that ain't just the best you can do?" he shot back.

Tomas's lean face twisted with anger as Longarm turned his own tactic against him. He cursed in Spanish and sprang forward, slashing viciously at Longarm's face. Longarm flung up the bowie to parry the attack. Sparks flew as the blades clashed stridently.

Suddenly, Longarm snapped a kick to Tomas's left knee. Tomas gasped in pain and surprise and stumbled backward, fighting to stay on his feet as his leg tried to fold up underneath him. Longarm seized the momentary advantage to press an attack of his own. Now it was all Tomas could do to fend off the slashes and thrusts of Longarm's blade.

Tomas ducked under a sweeping blow and with a shout of hate threw himself forward. He caught Longarm around the waist with one arm while trying to stab him in the kidneys with the other hand. Longarm went over backward, knocked off his feet by the tackle. Both men hit the ground, the impact jolting them apart.

Longarm rolled away quickly. Now, in addition to the wound on his arm, his leg and hip hurt like blazes where he had crashed to the ground. He came up on his left knee and saw Tomas several feet away, also struggling to rise.

"The hell with this," Longarm muttered. His arm whipped up and back, then flashed forward as he threw the knife in his hand.

It was a desperate gamble. He was unarmed now, and if Tomas avoided the throw, he could carve Longarm into little pieces at his leisure.

Tomas twisted, trying to get out of the way of the knife, but Longarm had put all of his speed and power behind the throw. The blade smacked into Tomas's chest just below his right shoulder. The vaquero screamed thinly and slumped to the side, dropping his own knife as he pawed at the handle of the Bowie. The blade had embedded itself deeply, and it didn't want to come free.

Longarm was on his feet by now. He kicked Tomas in the face, sending him flying backward to land in a limp sprawl. The bowie still jutted up from his shoulder. The wound was not a fatal one, but Tomas wouldn't be using his right arm normally anytime soon, if ever again.

Longarm turned away from his unconscious opponent and faced Harrigan. The circle of vaqueros had fallen silent, their cheers and shouts abruptly dying away to nothing.

Harrigan gestured at Tomas and said to Longarm, "You're not going to kill him?"

"No need," Longarm said with a shake of his head. "I reckon you've seen what I can do, Harrigan."

"I haven't seen you handle a gun yet."

Longarm smiled faintly. "You can give me back my Colt and try me for yourself, if you want."

Harrigan laughed. "I don't think so." He looked at his men. "Pepe, you and Juan take Tomas back to the bunkhouse and patch him up. And bring me my bowie when you get it out of him!"

"Si, patron," one of the men muttered as he and a companion sprang to follow Harrigan's orders.

Harrigan turned back to Longarm. He took the Colt he had tucked behind the sash around his waist and opened the cylinder, spilling the cartridges into the palm of his other hand. Then he extended the gun butt-first to Longarm.

"I'll feel better if this is unloaded for a while," Harrigan went on. "At least until you've come in the hacienda and had a drink with me."

Longarm nodded as he took the Colt and slipped it back into its holster. "Sounds good to me."

He started walking toward the main house with Harrigan at his side. So far he had seen no sign of Peter Braddock here on the ranch. From what he had seen and heard

110

back at the bushwhackers' camp, Longarm thought that Braddock intended to spend the night there. But if that wasn't the case, and if Braddock and Harrigan knew each other, as it had sounded when Braddock was talking to the gunmen, then Braddock could conceivably show up here at any time. That would be the end of Longarm's masquerade.

He would play that hand when it was dealt, Longarm decided. Every minute he was alive and free was a minute when fortune could swing back around to his side.

"Mescal?"

"Fine," Longarm replied.

Harrigan poured the drinks from a jug into tin cups. There was nothing fancy about the place, no feminine touches. The furniture was made of thick, rough-hewn beams. The dominant feature in the room was a massive fireplace. This was a man's room, strictly utilitarian.

"Salud," Harrigan said, then threw back his drink.

Longarm swallowed the thick, sweetish concoction and felt its fire blaze up in his belly. He drew strength from it.

Harrigan lifted the jug. "Another?"

Longarm shook his head. "Too much of that stuff on an empty stomach muddles a man's mind. I don't reckon that'd be too good an idea right now, since we ain't fully come to an understanding."

"I'm hiring you, aren't I?"

"Are you?" Longarm asked bluntly.

Harrigan matched his level stare, and after a moment the stocky redhead nodded. "I am. All hell's about to start poppin' down here, Parker, and I've got a hunch you'll be a good man to have on my side when that happens."

"What about that fella Tomas? I can't do a very good job of working for you if I have to keep looking over my shoulder all the time for him."

"You want me to get rid of him?" Harrigan shrugged.

"Consider it done. Some of the other boys won't like it very much, but what the hell."

"You don't have to get rid of him," Longarm said. "Just have a talk with him so he knows that he can't start skulking around trying to even the score. If he tries anything, I'll have to kill him. Fair enough?"

Harrigan poured himself another drink and nodded to Longarm over the brim of the cup. "Fair enough," he agreed.

Longarm sat down in a heavy chair covered with an Indian blanket, cocked his right ankle on his left knee, and took out the cheroot he had slipped in his pocket earlier. As he put it in his mouth, he said, "Tell me about this hombre Escobedo."

Harrigan sat down, too, and asked, "What about your arm? Don't you want somebody to patch it up?"

Longarm struck a match and held the lucifer to the tip of the cheroot. "It's just a scratch. It'll keep. What I want to know is what I'll have to do around here to earn my dinero."

"Whatever I say," Harrigan snapped. "Right now what I want you to do is stop Escobedo from bushwhacking my vaqueros."

"Escobedo's been ambushing your men?"

Harrigan waved a hand. "Not him personally, of course. But I figure that big *segundo* of his, a gent called Diablito, has had a hand in it. I've lost three men in the past six weeks."

"Bushwhacked?" Longarm asked with a frown.

"That's right. All three shot out of their saddles. Shot dead," Harrigan added bitterly.

Now that was mighty strange, Longarm thought. Three of Don Manuel's vaqueros had been ambushed recently, two killed and one badly wounded. From what Harrigan was saying, the same thing had happened over here as had taken place on Las Hermanas del Fuego.

Longarm rubbed his jaw. "I reckon you've struck back?"

"Not yet. You wouldn't know about this part of it . . ." Harrigan looked a little uncomfortable. "But I intend to marry the sister of Don Manuel Escobedo."

Longarm managed to put a look of surprise on his face. "You're courting the sister of the man you're having a range war with?"

"Damn it!" Harrigan slammed a fist down on the arm of the chair where he sat. "I don't want a range war. It's Escobedo! I won't deny that I've had some shady dealin's in the past, but this ranch ain't one of 'em. Not one head of cattle on my range has been rustled from anywhere else. Escobedo's the one who tries to throw a wide loop!"

Longarm didn't know what was more tired and battered, his body or his brain. Harrigan was telling the exact opposite story from what Don Manuel Escobedo claimed was going on around here. Both men blamed the other for all the troubles that seemed to be leading inevitably to a shooting war. Was Harrigan telling the truth? What reason would he have had to lie to a man he thought he was hiring to fight on his side?

Maintaining his calm demeanor, Longarm smoked in silence for a moment as he tried to sort out all the conflicting information he had learned today. As confusing as things were between Escobedo and Harrigan, they became even more muddled when Peter Braddock was thrown into the mix.

Harrigan stood up and began to pace back and forth. "Everything was all arranged for me to marry Escobedo's sister," he said. "A girl named Theresa . . . prettiest, sweetest gal you ever saw. But then Escobedo made some wild accusations about me poisoning one of his water holes, and I reckon I flew off the handle and told him to go to hell. He said the marriage was off."

"Sounds like the excitable type," Longarm commented.

"Not usually. Fact is, most of the time Don Manuel seems almost like he's half asleep. But when he gets a burr under his saddle . . ." Harrigan shook his head. "Anyway, he told me to get off his place. I didn't want any gunplay in front of Theresa, so I went along with what Escobedo said. But I came back later."

"And?" Longarm prodded, even though he was pretty sure he knew the answer.

Harrigan stopped his pacing and glared at Longarm. "I'm going to tell you something, Parker, and if it makes a difference, then the hell with you! We'll have it out right now!"

Longarm just looked at him and waited.

After a moment, Harrigan jerked his head toward the second floor of the hacienda. "She's up there."

"Who?" Longarm asked, playing along.

"Theresa. Escobedo's sister."

"You kidnapped her," Longarm said flatly.

"She was supposed to be my wife! I knew she still loved me. It was that . . . that damned brother of hers, poisonin' her against me—"

Harrigan broke off his explanation, shook his head, and resumed his pacing. "Nobody was hurt," he said. "I waited until there was nobody at the hacienda but Theresa and some of the servants. I got her to write a note to her brother, saying that she was going with me . . ."

That didn't jibe exactly with what Longarm had overheard in the room upstairs while he was on the roof, but it was close enough. Harrigan sounded like he had convinced himself that his version of the kidnapping was the truth.

"I'm going to make her understand," Harrigan said. "I know she still loves me. I'm going to make her see that things can still be the way they were supposed to." He threw a challenging look at Longarm, as if he had revealed more than he intended to. "So, does any of that make a difference to you, Parker?"

"Does it have any effect on how much you're going to pay me?" Longarm asked.

Harrigan blinked in surprise at the question. "No."

"Then it doesn't matter a damn to me what else you do, Harrigan."

Harrigan regarded him intently for a few seconds, then smiled. "I was right. You *are* a cold-nerved bastard."

Longarm put the cheroot back in his mouth, clamped his teeth on it, and smiled back at Harrigan.

Chapter 11

The sun had set well before Diablito returned to Las Hermanas del Fuego. The big man's craggy face was set in grim lines, and he had a body draped over the back of the horse in front of his saddle.

From where he was perched on the top rail of one of the corrals, Pablo saw Diablito riding in. He dropped easily to the ground and ran toward the main house, shouting, *"Patron! Patron!"*

Don Manuel Escobedo emerged from the hacienda, trailed by Dulcey and the elderly servant couple. Pablo saw the distracted look on Don Manuel's face and knew that the patron was once again in the grip of an evil spell cast by the woman who walked a few paces behind him. Pablo stopped running and stood still, watching Dulcey closely. When she glanced at him, he felt his soul tremble. No one ever believed the things he said about Dulcey, not Diablito or Esteban, not even the big American, Senor Custis. And certainly not Don Manuel, who had threatened Pablo with harsh punishment if he did not stop spreading lies about Dulcey.

But they were not lies, Pablo thought. She *was* a *bruja*. And she had Don Manuel in her power.

At this moment, however, the grim discovery that Diablito had made broke through the listlessness that all too often made Don Manuel slow of speech and thought. Diablito reined to a stop in front of the hacienda gate and swung down from his saddle. Then, as if the burden weighed little or nothing, he lifted the body from the back of the horse and stood there with it cradled gently in his arms.

"I found him in an arroyo on the edge of the desert," Diablito said thickly, his usually rumbling voice choked by emotion. "The others who rode with Esteban and Senor Custis lay near there. They were all dead."

"And the American?" Don Manuel asked.

Diablito shook his shaggy head. "I did not see him, or his horse. There was much blood in the arroyo. I think it came from Esteban, but some of it could have been from Senor Custis. Many tracks led down the arroyo. He could have gotten away, or the killers could have caught him and murdered him, too."

"Or taken him prisoner," Don Manuel muttered. "But why? Who would do such a thing?"

Dulcey spoke up. "You know, Don Manuel. This is the work of El Gordo. It must be."

Don Manuel's head jerked in a nod of agreement. "Yes," he said. "It had to be Harrigan's men. Again they have struck a blow to my heart!"

"And to mine," Diablito grunted. He looked down at the dead face of his friend Esteban, and as Pablo saw the need for vengeance that burned in Diablito's eyes, he thought it to be a terrible, wondrous thing.

Esteban and the others should have returned to the *rancho* late in the afternoon after escorting Senor Custis to the border. When they had not arrived, Diablito had grown worried and ridden out to look for them. Several hours had passed since then. Now it was night, and Esteban and the other vaqueros were dead, and although Pablo hated to agree with Dulcey about anything, he knew that she was right: Gordo Harrigan had the blood of these

117

men on his hands, whether he had actually pulled the trigger or not.

Don Manuel clenched his hands into fists and pressed them to his temples. "I must do something about this," he said, anguish in his voice. "But what? What?"

"Kill Harrigan and all of his men," Diablito said. "Now. Tonight."

Don Manuel looked up at his *segundo*. "You mean we should make war on Harrigan?"

Dulcey came forward a step. "Diablito is right, *patron*. The fat one would not expect it tonight. You can wipe him out."

"I . . . I do not know," Escobedo said with a shake of his head.

"I do," Diablito said. "They are dogs who deserve no mercy. They are worse than dogs, worse even than coyotes. We should ride to Harrigan's ranch with death in our hands."

"Death," Don Manuel murmured. He began to nod slowly. "Yes, death is what they deserve."

Still holding Esteban's body in his arms, Diablito turned toward the vaqueros who had come out of the bunkhouse to see what was going on. He bellowed, "Saddle the horses! Tonight, we ride!"

Pablo crossed himself and uttered a silent prayer for the safety of his friends.

The hoofbeats sounded like thunder as the riders approached the pass. Before they reached the gap in the ridge, Diablito reined in and lifted a hamlike hand in a signal to stop. He was in the lead, but Don Manuel Escobedo was close behind him. Diablito had argued that Don Manuel should stay behind at the hacienda, but the patron had refused to listen to reason. And the patron, after all, was the patron. His word had to be obeyed, even if he was a mere shell of the man he had once been.

Diablito turned in the saddle and looked at the large group of men behind him. More than two dozen vaqueros

118

had ridden out with him and Don Manuel. Every able-bodied man on the ranch had joined the party headed for Harrigan's. Each of them wanted vengeance on El Gordo for what had been done. For weeks the bad feelings had grown stronger and stronger, and today's atrocity had made a peaceful solution impossible. The only way to cleanse the stain on the honor of Las Hermanas del Fuego was with blood and fire.

"We must go slower now," Diablito called, softening his normally loud tones. Still, no one in the group had any trouble hearing him. "El Gordo may have sentries out. We cannot allow the sound of our horses to warn them of our coming."

Don Manuel nodded his agreement. "Diablito is right," he said. His voice was a little stronger now, and his thinking seemed clearer. "Surprise is on our side. We must keep it there."

"But, *patron*," one of the men said, "will this Harrigan not expect us? He had our friends murdered, if he did not commit the foul deed himself. Surely he knows we will strike back at him."

"He will not be expecting us so soon, nor in such numbers," Don Manuel said.

That was what Diablito thought, too, but he had to admit to himself that he was not completely convinced. If he had killed some of Harrigan's men, he would have been doubly alert for the possibility of retaliation. Diablito's anger had made him call out for immediate action, and Don Manuel had agreed. Now, there was a nagging doubt in the back of Diablito's mind. Perhaps it would have been better to wait.

No, that would only give Harrigan more time to prepare for them, another part of him argued. Best to strike quickly, before the enemy had time to get ready. That was always an excellent rule to follow.

Silently, Diablito waved for the riders to follow him and urged his horse into a walk. Once they were through the pass, there would be no turning back.

But really, they had already reached that point, Diablito realized. As soon as he had seen Esteban's bullet-riddled body lying at the bottom of that arroyo, he had known that his vengeance would not be denied.

And when he took that vengeance, it would be with great joy in his heart.

Pablo had trouble getting to sleep. He tossed and turned on the pile of hay in the barn that served as his bed. He was both excited and worried that Don Manuel and all the other men had gone to wage war on the one called Harrigan. He wished he could have gone with them. But none of the boys had been allowed to accompany the vaqueros, and while Pablo had considered chasing after them, he knew he could never keep up on foot.

With his eyes open wide, he sat up at the soft sound of a footstep. A shape loomed up in the darkness in the aisle of the barn. As it came slowly toward him, Pablo crossed himself and murmured, *"Jesus, Maria y Jose."*

"Pablo," a voice whispered.

Pablo caught his breath and scooted backward on his rump as fast as he could go, until his back bumped against the wall. Still, the dark shape seemed to float toward him, and the voice said again, "Pablo," calling his name like a demon summoning lost souls to *El Infierno*.

The shape moved into a patch of moonlight that filtered through an open window up in the loft, and in the silvery glow, the thick, curly, reddish-brown hair looked black as it fell around Dulcey's face. She said, "Pablo, what's wrong? It's only me."

His feet scrabbled against the hard-packed earth of the barn floor, as if he were trying to push himself through the adobe wall at his back to get away from her. Dulcey came closer, and Pablo let out a strangled cry. She leaned over, her hands reaching out for him.

"Do not fight me, Pablo. I want to help you."

Suddenly, he lunged to his feet and tried to dart past her. Dulcey moved quickly and caught hold of his shoulders. He cried out again and thrashed in her grip, but she was too strong for him. Steadily, she drew him toward her, and her arms went around him and held him tightly. He was pressed against her. He trembled like a deer.

Then, slowly, his shaking ceased. His harsh, rapid breathing slowed. "There," Dulcey said. "It is not such a bad thing to have me hold you, is it, Pablo?"

Tentatively, he raised his arms and put them around her waist. His head rested against her belly below the thrust of her breasts. She stroked his black hair and murmured words of comfort. Pablo began to cry.

"Hush now," Dulcey whispered. "It is all right. No one will harm you. But you must come with me into the house. You will be safe there."

At last, Pablo found his voice again. "S-safe?" he repeated. "Safe from what?"

Dulcey raised her head and looked along the aisle of the barn, through the open doors at the darkness. "There are bad things loose in the night," she said. "Come now. We must hurry."

Pablo went with her. No longer could he understand why he had been so afraid of her. Dulcey only wanted to take care of him, to protect him from whatever evil was abroad this night.

Side by side, hand in hand, they ran from the barn toward the hacienda. Pablo heard racing hoofbeats, soft at first but rapidly growing louder as they approached. Dulcey tugged on his hand to hurry him along. They dashed through the gate into the outer courtyard, and Dulcey slammed it shut behind them and locked it.

The riders swept down on the ranch a moment later. The horses pounded into the yard between the main house and the barns. In the darkness, the men were only vague shapes, but starlight winked off the barrels of the guns they held in their hands. "Spread out," their leader growled. "I want the place surrounded."

As the invaders began following the commands, the leader swung down from his saddle and strode over to the

121

gate. He took hold of the wrought iron and rattled it. An ancient padlock held the gate closed. The man lifted his revolver and fired twice, flame geysering from the muzzle. The lock leaped in the air, blasted loose from the hasp. The man jerked the gate open and stalked through it into the outer courtyard of the hacienda.

From the door of the house came a quavering voice. It called, *"Alto, hombre!"* The leader of the invaders ignored the warning and walked toward the house. The old man who, along with his wife, had served the Escobedo family for many, many years, stepped out of the shadows and pointed a shotgun at the intruder.

The pistol in the man's hand blasted before the elderly servant could pull the triggers of the shotgun. The old man cried out in pain as the bullet smacked into his chest and threw him backward. The shotgun fell from his hands and clattered to the ground. The jarring impact tripped one of the cocked triggers. That barrel went off with a dull boom, but the charge of buckshot drove harmlessly into the dirt.

The wounded man writhed on his back. With a scream, his wife ran out of the house and fell to her knees at his side. She clutched at him for a moment, then buried her hands in her hair under her shawl and ripped some of it out as she wailed in grief.

The gunman started past her, paying little attention. The wailing woman, still on her knees, lurched toward him and grappled with him, clawing at his legs. The man snarled a curse and swung the pistol at her head in a vicious backhand. The brutal blow sent her sprawling on the ground next to her husband, who was no longer moving. Other than a brief jerking of one leg under the shapeless dress, the old woman didn't move, either.

The leader of the invaders went on into the house, not looking behind him. He knew if there was any more trouble outside, his men could handle it.

As a matter of fact, there was a flurry of gunshots as the man searched through the hacienda, but it ended quickly. No one had been left at Las Hermanas del Fuego except the old house servants, the middle-aged blacksmith whose withered leg kept him from riding, and a few boys.

And the beautiful young woman. *She* was here somewhere.

The man found her, along with a boy who she pushed behind her skirts, in a room on the second floor that opened onto the balcony overlooking the inner courtyard. "Might as well come out," he told her. He had taken a silver candle holder from one of the rooms downstairs, a heavy thing of great beauty and value, and lit the candle to give him light for his search. Now the faint glow showed the young woman standing against the far wall of the room, her chin held high in defiance. She was every bit as beautiful as the man had been told.

"The boy is not to be harmed," she said, an imperious tone in her voice as if she were accustomed to being in command at all times.

The gunman shrugged. "There has been enough killing for one night, I suppose. As long as the boy causes no trouble, he will not be hurt. Neither will you. Now come downstairs."

Pablo looked up at Dulcey, waiting to see what she was going to do. Since his fear of her had disappeared out there in the barn, he quickly had grown to trust her, to depend on her. She would know what to do to make the bad man go away and leave them alone.

But instead, she nodded her agreement with what the man was saying, and she put her hand on Pablo's shoulder and squeezed hard as she said, "Come, Pablo. We must do as he says."

"No!" he exclaimed involuntarily.

Her fingers tightened even more on his shoulder, until he almost cried out in pain. "Yes," she said, her voice quiet. "We must."

He knew it would do no good to argue. Choking back a sob of anger and terror, he nodded and let Dulcey steer him toward the door. The gunman laughed and moved back. His wide-brimmed hat cast grotesque shadows in the flickering light of the candle he held.

Don Manuel and Diablito and the other men would come back and set everything right, Pablo told himself as the gunman ushered them downstairs into the main room of the hacienda. They would not let this evil man triumph.

But as he saw the light spilling through the open door and washing over the bodies lying outside, Pablo began to sense something that he had never really understood before. Sometimes evil was so strong, there was nothing even good men could do to stop it.

And this fair-haired American who had led the raid on Las Hermanas del Fuego was the most evil man Pablo had ever seen.

It seemed to Longarm that he had just stretched out on the bed and closed his eyes when the shouts and the gun-fire jolted him out of his sleep.

He rolled out of bed and came up on his feet. His Colt was in his hand instantly, jerked from the holster lying on the chair next to the bed. After the conversation he and Harrigan had had earlier, Harrigan had told him to reload the weapon, so the revolver had the usual five cartridges in it, the hammer resting on an empty chamber.

In bare feet and the bottom half of his underwear, Longarm went to the window and peered out at the night. Harrigan had given him a room in the house, thinking that after what Longarm had done to Tomas, it might not be a good idea to have him bunk with the vaqueros. He saw a rider race by in the shadows. Flame gushed from the barrel of a gun as the horseman snapped a shot at the house. Longarm ducked back as the slug thudded into the adobe wall only inches from the window.

Longarm had caught a glimpse of the rider in the backwash from the muzzle flash. The look had lasted only a fraction of a heartbeat, but Longarm would have sworn that the rider was Diablito.

More shots rattled outside, and they were answered by

the sharp cracks of rifles from the hacienda and the bunk-house. It sounded like a small-scale war going on out there. Were Don Manuel Escobedo's men invading Harrigan's ranch? Had Don Manuel found out about the ambush that had taken the lives of Esteban and the other men and come here to seek vengeance for them?

It seemed to Longarm that the most likely answer to both questions was yes. Nothing short of an all-out attack would have produced such a ruckus.

Now the question was, what was he going to do about it?

The first thing he decided was to get his pants on. When he had done that, he shrugged into a shirt, stomped into his boots, and strapped his shell belt around his waist. Moving quickly, Longarm was out of his room in a little over a minute after the shooting had roused him.

"Parker!"

Longarm turned to see Gordo Harrigan running toward him, a Winchester in each hand. Harrigan tossed one of the rifles to him. Longarm caught it deftly.

"It's Escobedo and his bunch!" Harrigan said as he paused to catch his breath. He grinned. "You're going to get to earn some of your pay in a hurry."

"What are they after?" Longarm asked. "The girl?"

Harrigan shrugged. "How the hell do I know? They tried to sneak up on the place, but one of the guards spotted them and got off a couple of shots before they gunned him down." He laughed. "They're fools if they think they can root us out of here! The walls are a foot thick. This house was built to withstand attacks by Yaquis and bandits."

Longarm knew Harrigan might be right. Behind thick adobe walls, firing through narrow rifle slits, the defenders could hold off a superior attacking force for a long time. The biggest questions were food and water. If Harrigan had plenty of both—and Longarm had no reason to suspect that he didn't—then this ill-advised attack almost certainly was doomed to failure.

"Come on!" Harrigan urged. "Pick your spot, Parker, and ventilate some of those bastards!"

Longarm wasn't just about to shoot any of Escobedo's vaqueros, not until he had the straight of all this. Everything was tangled up like one of those Mexican cattle brands that resembled nothing so much as a skillet full of snakes. He jerked his head toward the second floor and said, "What about Senorita Escobedo? Shouldn't somebody watch out for her?"

"She'll be fine," Harrigan snapped. "I closed the shutters over her windows. No bullets can get through to where she is. Now come on, Parker! Let's get to work!"

Longarm had no choice but to run down the hall with Harrigan to the main room of the hacienda. They went to rifle slits on either side of the door, Harrigan to the left and Longarm to the right. It was dark in the room, the lamps having been blown out so that the defenders could see to aim better.

Longarm slid the barrel of the Winchester through the narrow opening. He fired as a rider raced by outside. The bullet went high, though, just as Longarm intended. He levered another cartridge into the chamber and looked for another target.

Over the next ten minutes, Longarm did some of the best shooting he had ever done—and didn't hit a thing. He placed his shots carefully, so that no one could tell he was missing on purpose. His bullets went high, low, and wide, but not by much. In the dust and noise and confusion, it was entirely possible that anyone watching him would have believed that he downed several of the attackers.

Unfortunately, no one else was aiming to miss, and Escobedo's men had ridden right into a hornet's nest. Longarm saw several of them fall, shot out of their saddles. The ones who weren't killed right away but only wounded were riddled by the defenders almost as soon as they hit the ground.

Longarm was shocked when he spotted Escobedo himself on a big black horse, firing a pistol toward the house as the horse reared on its hind legs. On the other side of the door, Harrigan yelled, "There's the bastard himself! I'll get him!" He slammed two shots from the rifle in his hands.

Both slugs must have missed, because Escobedo wheeled his mount and bounded away, seemingly unharmed. He was waving and calling to his men. Longarm thought he was ordering them to retreat. The attack had failed, and even someone as blinded by hate as Don Manuel could see that.

But the Escobedo riders weren't quite through, especially Diablito. Longarm saw the big *segundo* whirl past the house on horseback, and he threw something in his hand toward the hacienda. Longarm saw sparks flying through the air and realized that Diablito had just thrown a stick of dynamite at them, and the fuse was burning.

"Dynamite!" Longarm shouted. He dropped the rifle and flung himself toward Harrigan, wrapping his arms around the startled man and diving to the floor with him. "Get down!"

Longarm had seen close up what dynamite could do. The thunderclap of the explosion sounded like it was right outside the house, just on the other side of the wall. The blast was so loud that Longarm was half-deafened. Something smashed into his back, jarring a groan out of him. Then, more debris pelted down around him. Dust clogged his throat and made him choke and cough. As his hearing began to come back, he heard more shots, but they were fading away in the distance.

Something stirred underneath him. Longarm realized he was lying on top of Gordo Harrigan, and what felt like half the wall was pressing down on him from above. He arched his back and lifted, and some of the weight fell away. Still coughing, Longarm shoved pieces of shattered adobe off him and staggered to his feet. He looked down at Harrigan. The man wasn't moving, and blood formed a black streak across his forehead where something had struck him. He was alive, though. Longarm could hear his harsh breathing.

But with Harrigan out cold, this was his chance to get out of here, Longarm thought. There was so much confusion everywhere that if he could get his hands on a horse, he could take off for the tall and uncut without anyone being the wiser. He hated to leave Theresa Escobedo behind, but if he could join forces again with her brother, maybe he could figure out a way to get her back that would work better than this frontal attack had.

The dynamite had blown a gaping hole in the wall of the hacienda. Longarm stepped through it. A second later he had vanished into the shadows.

Chapter 12

Longarm made a wide circle toward the barns and the corrals. He hoped to find the dun he had been riding earlier, but he would settle for any good horse that would carry him away from Harrigan's ranch.

It was hard to believe that only that morning he had picked out the dun from Don Manuel's remuda. So much had happened since then. A glance at the stars told him he had slept perhaps two hours before the attack awakened him. That was nowhere near enough rest, but it would have to do.

He could still hear hoofbeats in the distance. That would be Don Manuel and his men, retreating toward the ridge that separated the two valleys. Longarm thought hc could catch up to them before they reached the Escobedo ranch, if he could get his hands on a horse without too much delay.

Unfortunately, as he rounded a corner of the corral, he ran into someone, just as he had earlier in the evening when he was trying to get away the first time.

Longarm heard the quickly indrawn breath as the man got ready to shout a warning. The big lawman's left hand shot out and clamped around the throat of the vaquero, choking off the outcry. At the same time, Longarm palmed out his Colt and smacked the barrel against the man's skull. The high-peaked sombrero crumpled, taking some of the force of the blow. The man still struggled. Longarm had to hit him again before he went limp and slumped to the ground.

Grimacing in frustration, Longarm hurried on toward the nearest barn. He heard shouts coming from the hacienda itself and wondered if some of the men had found Harrigan under the collapsed wall. Would they notice that he was gone? Would they even know that he had been there with Harrigan unless El Gordo woke up and told them? Longarm hoped that he would have at least a few minutes to get away before anybody realized that he was missing.

He heard a familiar whinny and looked into the corral to see the dun moving around skittishly with several other horses. "Glad to see you, old son," Longarm said softly. He climbed quickly to the top rail and paused there for a second. After all the shooting, the horses were nervous. If he went into the corral, they might attack him. But he had to run that risk, because his time was slipping away. He dropped to the ground inside the fence.

The other horses shied away, but the dun stood there, nostrils flaring, seemingly challenging Longarm to come and get him. "Take it easy," Longarm told the horse as he approached. He held out a hand. "You remember me, don't you?"

The dun nipped at Longarm's hand, forcing him to jerk it back to avoid the slashing teeth. The sudden movement made the horse dance back and rear up. It pawed at the air with its front hooves.

As the dun came down, Longarm darted forward and caught hold of its ear. He tangled his other hand in the animal's mane. The dun tried to jerk away, but Longarm held on firmly. "Stop that," he said, his voice stern. "You behave yourself, you jughead."

The horse stood still then, trembling slightly. Longarm

130

didn't want to take the time to find a saddle. He had learned to ride bareback as a kid in West-by-God Virginia, and that was a skill one never forgot. He shifted his grip, leaped up, and swung a leg over the dun's back.

He could tell the horse didn't like it much, but the dun didn't start bucking or sunfishing. Guiding the mount with his knees and his grip on its mane, Longarm rode to the corral gate. He leaned over, lifted the rope loop that kept the gate closed, and pushed it open. He rode out, leaving the gate gaping wide behind him. If the other horses followed him, so much the better. A shortage of mounts would make it harder for Harrigan's men to pursue him if they decided to give chase.

Longarm walked the dun until he was well away from the corral, expecting at any second to hear a shout of alarm. The vaqueros were still too busy cleaning up the aftermath of the attack to pay any attention to him, however. When he judged that he was out of easy earshot, he nudged the dun with his knees and urged it into a trot.

He steered a course straight for the pass through the ridge. That was the way Don Manuel and the others had gone. Longarm hoped he was headed the right direction. He had never seen this valley by daylight and was unfamiliar with its landmarks. He could see the ridge, though, a long dark line against the starlit sky, and off to the side the twin peaks of the dormant volcanoes loomed much higher, blotting out many of the celestial guideposts. As long as he could see the Sisters of Fire, he could find his way around, Longarm decided.

He had ridden a couple of miles and was making his way up the slope toward the pass when a gunshot spurted at him from behind a rock. Longarm heard the bullet whip past his head. The dun leaped to the side, spooked by the blast, and Longarm struggled to bring the horse under control. At the same time, he yelled, "Don't shoot! I'm a friend, damn it!"

A startled voice came back at him. "Senor Custis? *Dios mio,* is that you?"

Longarm recognized Diablito's gravel-like tones. He heeled the dun ahead and called out, "*Hola*, Diablito!"

The massive *segundo* of Las Hermanas del Fuego stepped out from behind the rock. "I slipped away to guard our trail while Don Manuel led the rest of the men back to the ranch," he said.

"I figured as much."

"But I never expected to see you, Senor Custis! What are you doing here?"

"Following you and Don Manuel," Longarm explained. "I was back there at Harrigan's ranch when you raided the place."

The barrel of Diablito's rifle, which had been drooping toward the ground, started to come up again. "You were with El Gordo?" he asked suspiciously.

"I was a prisoner," Longarm said, deciding that to try to explain his short-lived masquerade as a hired gun for Harrigan would be too complicated right now. "I got away during the confusion of the battle." That much was true, at least.

Diablito lowered the rifle again, obviously accepting Longarm's answer. "We were afraid you were dead, murdered along with the others," he said. "But I knew that El Gordo's men might have captured you. Did he say why he had Esteban and the others killed?"

Longarm shook his head. Again, the complicated nature of the situation kept him from explaining that Harrigan had seemed unaware of the ambush that had taken the lives of Esteban and the rest of the vaqueros. Longarm had been too busy and too tired to devote much thought to the question, but as he turned it over in his mind now, he wondered why the bushwhackers had made camp up on the ridge instead of going to Harrigan's ranch. Clearly, there was a connection between them and Harrigan. They had spoken of El Gordo as if he were their employer.

Yet Harrigan was convinced that Don Manuel Escobedo's men had been ambushing his riders and poisoning his water holes. He blamed Don Manuel for all the troubles just as surely as Escobedo blamed him.

Longarm rubbed the back of his hand across his mouth. He would try to sort this out when he got back to Don Manuel's ranch. They could sit down and go through the whole thing then.

"Let's go," Longarm said. "From what I saw down there, Harrigan's men aren't going to be coming after you tonight."

Diablito laughed. "The dynamite, it made a big boom, no?"

Longarm didn't reveal how close he had been to that "big boom." He said, "It sure did."

Diablito retreated behind the rock and brought out his horse. He mounted up and took the lead. A short time later, he and Longarm galloped through the pass in the ridge. Not far down the slope on the other side, Don Manuel and the rest of the survivors from the ill-fated raid were waiting.

"Patron!" Diablito called out. "Look who I found. It is Senor Custis!"

"Senor!" Don Manuel said in surprise. "What are you doing here? We feared you were dead. It was to avenge you as much as the others that we rode to Harrigan's ranch tonight."

"I got bushwhacked just like Esteban and the others," Longarm said. "I got away for a while, then Harrigan grabbed me."

"Es verdad?"

Longarm thought he detected a hint of suspicion in Don Manuel's voice as he asked the question. "I'll explain the whole thing when we get back to the ranch."

"You no longer wish to return across the border to Texas?"

"When this trouble is over," Longarm said. "That'll be soon enough."

And, he added silently, when he had figured out what role Peter Braddock was playing here, and the fugitive was either in custody—or dead.

133

• • •

The trail led toward the Sisters of Fire. As he rode, Longarm looked up at the twin mountains, looming so darkly above the valley, and wondered how long it had been since they had erupted. It had been generations, he knew. Not even the oldest of the servants on the ranch remembered such a cataclysm. Yet everyone who lived in this region had to be aware of them. The possibility that the mountains would once again spew molten lava and deadly gases was small but could not be forgotten.

There were more immediate threats, however. Longarm wondered if it would be possible to get Don Manuel Escobedo and Gordo Harrigan to sit down together and talk about the violence that was plaguing both their ranges. Could it be that someone was trying to play both of them against each other for some unknown reason?

A meeting to talk peace was unlikely, considering the bad blood between the two men. There was also the matter of Theresa Escobedo to consider. Though he considered himself justified in doing so, Harrigan had kidnapped her and was holding her prisoner. Theresa's brother would not be able to just forget about that insult.

As if reading Longarm's mind as they rode side by side, Don Manuel asked, "While you were at El Gordo's hacienda, did you see . . . a young woman?"

"If you're talking about your sister, Don Manuel, I did see her, and she's fine."

"I am . . . pleased to hear that," Don Manuel said stiffly.

He thought that Theresa had gone away with Harrigan voluntarily, Longarm remembered. He didn't know the truth of the matter.

That was one thing that could be cleared up right now, Longarm decided. He said, "I'm not meaning to butt into family matters, Don Manuel, but there's something you ought to know about your sister and Harrigan."

"Please, senor, I do not want to hear—"

"Maybe you do," Longarm broke in. "You see, Senorita Theresa didn't go with Harrigan willingly. He kidnapped

134

her while the rest of you were away from the ranch."

Don Manuel reined in sharply, bringing his horse to a stop, and the rest of the group did likewise. He stared at Longarm in the darkness and said, "What?"

"Harrigan wanted you to think that Theresa chose to be with him, but that's not true. She's a prisoner in his hacienda just as much as I was. I'm sorry I didn't have a chance to set her free and bring her with me when I got away."

"But . . . but I do not understand," Escobedo muttered. "Dulcey told me . . . and there was a note from Theresa . . ."

"Dulcey must've been fooled by Harrigan's act, too. And, as for that note, I think Harrigan forced Theresa to write it, probably by threatening to kill some of the servants if she didn't cooperate with him."

"*Dios mio!*" Don Manuel crossed himself. "And all this time I thought . . . thought that Theresa . . ." He lifted a hand to his forehead and rubbed it as he closed his eyes. "*Ay,* it is so hard to think these days. But I am very pleased to know that my beloved sister did not betray me."

"I reckon you can put that worry out of your mind," Longarm assured him.

"That is very good to know, my friend."

Longarm's revelation about Theresa seemed to have erased the last bits of suspicion that Don Manuel might have had concerning him. It wasn't much, but as they rode on toward the ranch, Longarm felt that at least he had straightened out a little of the tangled web that lay over the mountains and deserts of northern Mexico.

A tinge of gray in the eastern sky told him that dawn was approaching. The past twenty-four hours had been packed so full of frenzied action it was difficult to believe that all of it had taken place in a single day. Longarm's body certainly knew that was the case. When they got back to the ranch, the first thing he wanted to do was sleep for about a week.

The lights of the hacienda came in view. "Dulcey and the others are waiting for us," Don Manuel murmured. Bitterness crept into his voice as he went on, "Fewer of us are returning than left last night."

Raiding Harrigan's ranch like that had been a foolish thing to do, but Longarm didn't think this was the time to point that out to Escobedo. Don Manuel already knew he had made a mistake that had cost the lives of several of his men. He would blame himself for that for a long time, and deservedly so.

They rode past the main house toward the barns and the corrals and the bunkhouse. As the horses plodded along in the pre-dawn grayness, Longarm thought he saw something move on top of the wall around the outer courtyard. His eyes narrowed and he looked again. He saw about four inches of a rifle barrel protruding over the adobe wall.

"Look out!" he called, instinct making the words leap from his throat. "It's a trap!"

For a split second, as he drove his boot heels into the dun's flanks and sent the horse leaping forward, he thought about how foolish he would look if he'd made a mistake in the bad light. But then shots began to blast out and muzzle flashes ripped holes in the curtain of darkness. A man yelled in pain.

Several ambushers were hidden along the wall of the hacienda's courtyard. All of them opened up at once in a volley that emptied a couple of saddles. Longarm, Don Manuel, and Diablito galloped side by side toward the corrals with the other vaqueros strung out behind them. If they could reach the shelter of one of the barns, they could fort up and make a fight of it. There was no time now to wonder who the hidden gunmen were. It was enough to know that they would have to fight for their lives.

But then lead and flame spat from the barns as well, and Diablito grunted and rocked back in the saddle. He managed to stay on his horse even though he was hit, and his hand came up with a pistol in it, blaring death.

Longarm kneed the dun into a turn. "They're in the barns, too!" he called as he rode along the front of one of the corrals. Don Manuel, Diablito, and the others followed. Longarm snapped a couple of shots toward the nearest barn, aiming at the muzzle flashes of the bushwhackers' guns. He didn't expect to hit anything, though, shooting from the back of a running horse.

The other vaqueros were putting up as much of a fight as they could, throwing wild shots here and there. But clearly they had ridden into a trap, and with guns all around them, their only chance was flight. Longarm urged all the speed he could get out of the dun and aimed for the creek that flowed a few hundred yards away.

More bullets sang their deadly song around his head, but he was unhit. He threw a glance over his shoulder and saw that Don Manuel, Diablito, and the rest of the riders were still with him, following his lead in this moment of crisis. Longarm wasn't sure who had appointed him ramrod of this bunch, but if that was the case, he'd do his best to lead them to safety.

Suddenly, Diablito's horse went down, falling so violently that Diablito was flung out of the saddle and went sailing through the air like some sort of gigantic bird. He crashed to the ground and rolled over several times before coming to a stop.

Longarm hauled back with one hand on the dun's mane to bring the horse to a halt, while using the hand that held his gun to wave the others on. "Head for the creek!" he shouted to Don Manuel. "Take cover in the trees! I'll get Diablito!"

By now, Longarm had seen the big *segundo* raise his head and shake it groggily. So he was still alive, even though he had been wounded in the initial volley of gunfire and had just been thrown off his horse. Longarm sent the dun running toward him.

"Diablito!" he shouted as he jammed his Colt back in its holster. "Hang on!"

Bullets kicked up dirt around the horse's hooves. Dirt was spouting around Diablito, too, as he pushed himself onto hands and knees. "Go back, Senor Custis!" he called. "Leave me!"

"The hell with that!" Longarm reached Diablito and whirled the dun in a turn. He reached down. "Come on!"

"The horse cannot carry us both!"

"Damn it!" Longarm snapped as a slug whined past his ear. "Get on here before they find the range!"

Diablito clasped his wrist, and Longarm pulled up with all his strength. Diablito scrambled onto the back of the dun behind him. Longarm kicked his heels and called out to the horse. The dun strained under the weight of the two big men but managed to break into a gallop. The horse had plenty of sand in its craw, that was for damned sure, Longarm thought.

They rode toward the creek, and gradually the firing died away behind them. When Longarm reached the cover of the cottonwoods that lined the banks of the stream, he called, "Don Manuel!"

"Here," Escobedo replied. He and several other riders loomed up out of the shadows under the trees. Despite the lightening of the sky, it would be dark here for quite a while yet.

Still, there was enough light for Longarm to be able to count the men who sat their horses there on the creek bank. He saw Don Manuel and seven other men. Counting himself and Diablito, that was ten. Seventeen riders had been in the party a few minutes earlier as they approached the hacienda. That meant they had lost seven men in the ambush.

Longarm's belly clenched in sick anger. Would the killing never stop? Who had set this trap for them, whose fingers had pulled the triggers of the guns that had lain in wait?

Harrigan wasn't to blame for this. There was no way El Gordo could have reached the ranch ahead of Longarm, Don Manuel and the others.

But there was one group of gunmen he couldn't account for, Longarm recalled. He had thought that the men who'd ambushed him and Esteban and the other vaqueros the day before were settling down for the night in their camp on the ridge. But he couldn't be certain that was what had happened. They might have sat around and drank for a while, then rode out again, bent on some other murderous errand.

Those thoughts flashed through Longarm's brain in a matter of seconds, and as they did, Escobedo said, "Who did this? Who lays in wait for me in my own home?"

His voice broke as he asked the anguished questions. The man was in a bad way, Longarm realized, pushed to the breaking point by everything that had happened, especially the deaths of his men. Longarm had been pushed physically almost beyond endurance, but at least he didn't have to carry the emotional burdens that Don Manuel did.

Longarm felt sorry for Don Manuel, but he was more concerned right now with Diablito. The *segundo* had at least one bullet in him. Longarm grasped Diablito's arm and helped him slide to the ground, then dismounted and stood beside him. "How bad are you hit, *amigo?*" he asked.

"A mere scratch, that is all," Diablito declared. But even though he was on his feet, he was swaying a little, and when he pulled back his *charro* jacket, the white shirt beneath it was dark with blood on the right side.

Longarm gripped his arm to keep him from falling. "You'd better sit down," he said. "There's a deadfall over there. That'll do."

Diablito wanted to argue, but Longarm got him settled on the fallen log. Turning to Don Manuel, Longarm said, "Somebody better get that jacket and shirt off him and see about patching up that bullet hole before he bleeds to death."

Don Manuel just sat on his horse, staring straight ahead and not saying anything.

Longarm bit back a curse. Obviously, Don Manuel

wasn't going to be a damned bit of good right now. Long-arm was going to have to tend to Diablito and then see if he could figure out what the hell to do about the fact that the ranch had been taken over by gunmen.

Before he could do anything, three shots sounded, and a voice shouted, "Hey, down there at the creek! Don Manuel! Are you there, Escobedo? We need to parley!"

Longarm's spine stiffened, and his face twisted in a grimace of hate and anger. He knew that voice, knew who it belonged to.

Peter Braddock.

Chapter 13

Pablo heard all the shooting from where he sat in the kitchen of the hacienda with Dulcey. From time to time he began to tremble. He didn't know what it all meant, but he knew it could not be good. The American and the other invaders who had taken over the ranch were killing someone out there, just as they had killed the old man and the old woman earlier in the night.

"Don't worry, little one," Dulcey said, reaching across the table to take hold of Pablo's hand. "It will be all right. You will not be harmed."

"The . . . the bad men . . ." Pablo gasped out in his fear.

"They will not hurt you," Dulcey said. "I will see to that."

He took little comfort from her bold words. She was as much a prisoner of the invaders as he was, as powerless in the hands of these ruthless men who killed to seize what they wanted. But she seemed to be waiting for some sort of response from him, so he summoned up a weak smile and nodded his head. Dulcey smiled back at him and squeezed his hand.

Outside the shooting went on for a long time before it finally stopped . . .

● ● ●

Longarm stepped over to the horse on which Don Manuel
was still mounted and clasped the rancher's wrist. "Don
Manuel!" he said sharply, knowing that he had to break
through the stunned reverie that gripped the man. "Listen
to me! You have to talk to that son of a bitch who's
calling you."

Don Manuel shook his head. "I . . . I cannot. You do it,
Senor Custis—"

"I can't," Longarm broke in. "He can't know I'm down
here with you."

Diablito heaved himself up from the deadfall and stumbled over to put a heavy hand on Longarm's shoulder.
"Who is this man, Senor Custis?"

Longarm looked around at the big *segundo*. "The bastard who dumped me in the river in Santa Elena Canyon.
He's a fugitive from American law." Longarm took a deep
breath, then plunged ahead, knowing it would no longer
serve any purpose to keep his true identity a secret. "I'm
a deputy United States marshal. That gent's name is Peter
Braddock, and he knows I'm after him."

Diablito swayed a little, and Longarm knew that the
hand on his shoulder might be all that was keeping Diablito on his feet. "A gringo lawman," Diablito rumbled.
"But this is Mexico . . ."

"I know, I don't have any legal authority down here.
So look at it this way. You folks saved my life, starting
with young Pablo. I owe you that debt. I'll fight alongside
you as a friend, not as a lawman."

The hand on his shoulder squeezed harder. *"Amigo,"*
Diablito said. "Truly, you are, Senor Custis. But why do
you wish this man Braddock not to know you are here
with us?"

"I'm not sure what he wants to parley about, but he'll
never trust you if he knows I've thrown in with you.
Maybe you can stall him, play for time, if he doesn't
know about me."

Diablito nodded. "I would talk to him, senor, but . . . I am feeling a bit tired . . ."

With no more warning than that, Diablito's hand slipped from Longarm's shoulder and he folded up, collapsing onto the ground like a puppet with its strings cut.

That seemed to get through to Don Manuel more than Longarm had been able to. Escobedo leaned forward in his saddle and said anxiously, "Diablito? *Madre de Dios*, someone must care for him—"

"Esbobedo!" Braddock was shouting toward the creek again. "Damn it, you'd better talk to me!"

Longarm motioned for a couple of the surviving vaqueros to tend to Diablito, then he slipped toward the edge of the trees and knelt behind one of them. In the growing light, he saw a small hummock of ground about a hundred yards away. Someone was standing behind it holding up a pole with a white rag tied to it. Longarm knew Braddock and some of the other bushwhackers had to be hidden back there.

A step sounded beside him. Don Manuel strode up, looking a little stronger and more aware of his surroundings now. Longarm had no idea how long that mental clarity would last this time, but he hoped it would be long enough for them to find out what was going on here.

"Don't use Braddock's name when you parley with him," Longarm hissed. "You're not supposed to know who he is."

Don Manuel nodded his understanding. He raised his voice and called out, "I hear you, gringo! What do you want of me?"

"Escobedo?"

"I am Don Manuel Escobedo. I ask again, what do you want?"

Longarm heard a faint burst of arrogant laughter from Braddock. It made him tighten his jaw and narrow his eyes. Sooner or later, Braddock would get what was coming to him.

"I want your word of honor that you and the men you

have left will ride away from here and never return!" Braddock called. "This ranch is mine now!"

Longarm saw Don Manuel stiffen in outrage. "This land has been in the Escobedo family for generations!" he shouted back. "It will never belong to a . . . a thief and a killer!"

Again, Braddock laughed. "That's where you're wrong, Don Manuel. I've got enough guns to hold the place against an army. And I have hostages—a mighty pretty gal, for one!"

"Dulcey," Don Manuel breathed in horror. "Dulcey in the hands of that swine . . ." He buried his face in his hands and cried out a muffled, "No!"

Staying out of sight behind the tree trunk, Longarm gripped Escobedo's arm. "Steady, Don Manuel," he said. "He hasn't hurt Dulcey, or he wouldn't be trying to use her to convince you to give in."

That wasn't necessarily true, but Longarm didn't elaborate. Right now he had to keep Don Manuel thinking as clearly as possible.

"I've got a boy called Pablo, too," Braddock went on, "and some other kids and servants. I'll kill every damn one of 'em unless you go along with what I'm asking, Escobedo! Their blood will be on your head!"

Don Manuel was breathing heavily and raggedly. He turned his head to look at Longarm. "I . . . I do not know what to do . . ."

"Tell him you'll do what he says."

Don Manuel stared at him. "Abandon my ranch? Give that gringo Las Hermanas del Fuego?"

"A promise made to a man of no honor carries no weight," Longarm said.

"A man's word is his word," Don Manuel argued. "No matter to whom he gives it."

Longarm bit back a curse of frustration. He had dealt with these *grandes* and their inflated sense of honor before. Longarm considered himself an honest man, and when he made a promise, he kept it—unless it was made

144

to no-account, murdering scum like Braddock.

"Right now we're just trying to keep Dulcey and Pablo and the others alive," Longarm said. "Can't you understand that, Don Manuel?"

For a few seconds, Don Manuel just stared at him. Then, slowly, he began to nod his head. "You are right," he said dully. "All that matters is their lives."

He faced the hummock again and shouted, "We will do as you say! My men and I will ride away from here!"

"I have your word of honor on that, Escobedo?" Braddock called mockingly.

Longarm saw Don Manuel's hands clench into fists. "My word of honor," he said, then repeated it loudly enough for Braddock to hear.

"Good! You take the trail on the other side of the creek and ride out of the valley where we can see you! We'll have field glasses on you the whole time. If you turn back, we'll start killing the hostages! You've got five minutes to get started!"

Don Manuel turned away, unable to say anything else. He stumbled over to the creek, where Diablito was sitting again on the deadfall, conscious as one of the vaqueros wrapped strips of torn shirt around his bloody torso to bind the bullet-furrow in his side.

Longarm followed and said, "Better get mounted up in a hurry. We don't have much time."

Diablito looked up at him. The big man's face was pale, but his dark eyes still held plenty of strength. "I heard the gringo say he would be watching with field glasses. Will he not see you and recognize you as we ride out, Senor Custis?"

Longarm shook his head. "Nope, because I'm not leaving. Don Manuel didn't make any promises that I wouldn't stay behind and try to turn the tables on that bastard."

Escobedo's head was drooping again, but it came up at Longarm's words. "What can you do? They are many.

145

You heard what the American said. He can hold the hacienda against an army."

"Sometimes," Longarm said, "one man can go places and do things an army can't."

Longarm was convinced now the force that had taken over the hacienda was the same one that had bushwhacked the group heading for the border the day before. Braddock's presence was evidence enough of that. The bushwhackers numbered about a dozen. Twelve to one, he mused as he stayed hidden in the trees along the creek and watched Don Manuel and the others ride away. He supposed he had faced worse odds at times during his eventful career—but right now he couldn't remember just when.

The sky over the ridge to the east was a mixture of orange and pale blue. The sun was not up yet, but it would be before much longer. If he was going to have a chance to slip into the hacienda, it would have to be soon, before the light of a new day washed over the valley.

Brush grew thickly along the banks of the creek. Longarm left his dun where it was, cropping contentedly on thick grass after its long night of work, and made his way along the stream, using every bit of cover he could find. He was more heavily armed now. He had the Colt Don Manuel had given him the day before, plus another revolver and a bowie knife tucked behind his belt. He carried a fully-loaded Winchester in one hand. He was loaded for bear, he thought with a wry grin, but what he was really after was coyote.

A two-legged coyote named Braddock.

Longarm followed the creek at least half a mile before he ventured out from the brush and began circling around the hacienda. He glanced back and spotted Don Manuel and the other riders climbing one of the mountain trails in plain sight. The sun was already hitting there and reflecting brightly off the silver *conchas* that decorated their clothing and saddles. Without really thinking about it, Longarm counted the riders and came up with eight.

There should have been nine.

He froze behind a bush and counted again. Eight riders were leaving the valley. It wasn't hard to tell who was missing. None of the men Longarm could see were big enough to be Diablito.

Had the *segundo* passed out from his wound or even died? Or had he doubled back?

Longarm shook his head. He didn't have time to check on Diablito. All he could do was hope for the best.

He kept circling, taking advantage of every bit of cover he could find, until he was able to come at the hacienda from the side opposite the creek. The place looked quiet and peaceful now. No one would ever know by looking at it that it had been the site of a pitched battle an hour earlier.

The sun began to peek over the ridge as Longarm moved in. This whole effort might be futile, might accomplish nothing other than getting him killed. But he couldn't turn back now. His anger and his hatred of Peter Braddock drove him on. As a lawman, he'd had to learn not to give in to his emotions and let them rule him. But there were times when hate was about all a man had left, and this was one of them.

He headed for a small stone building that was used as a smokehouse. Crouching behind it, he was hidden from the hacienda. He edged an eye around the corner. He saw, past the corral, the tunnel that led to the inner courtyard. The gate was closed but didn't appear to be locked. No guards were in sight. In fact, the place looked deserted. Longarm knew that wasn't true. It was full of gunmen who would kill him in the blink of an eye if they got the chance. It was his job now to see that they didn't get that chance.

No one moved at any of the windows, but there could be watchers inside. Braddock wasn't a careless man. Longarm took a deep breath and knew he would have to risk it. He darted out from behind the smokehouse and headed for the corral, crouching low so that the horses and the poles of the enclosure itself would shield him from view to a certain extent.

He reached the corner of the corral, paused for a second, then ran toward the hacienda. Reaching it without incident, he flattened himself against the wall next to the tunnel gate, the Winchester held slanted across his chest. He stood there for a long moment, breathing deeply again, and listened. No outcry sounded, no shouts of alarm at the sight of an intruder. He had come this far without being seen. Now to get in the house . . .

Footfalls sounded inside the tunnel, echoing hollowly against the adobe walls.

Longarm stood absolutely still, waiting for the man who was approaching the gate. He had been right—the gate was pulled up but not locked. A moment later, the man who was coming reached it and pushed it open, stepping through into the sunlight.

Longarm struck like a coiled sidewinder, smashing the butt of the rifle against the side of the man's head. He both felt and heard the crunch of bone as the man's skull shattered under the blow. There had been no time for him to yell. The man went down in utter silence, dead even as he hit the ground.

Well, that was one of them, Longarm thought as he bent and grabbed the collar of the dead man's jacket. He hauled the corpse to the side where it couldn't be seen from inside the tunnel, then pressed his back to the wall again.

The hacienda was still quiet. No one had witnessed the brief incident of violence, Longarm thought. He waited a moment longer, then slipped through the gate which still stood open.

There were doors along both sides of the tunnel. Servants' quarters, Longarm recalled. All of them were closed. The survivors—the hostages—probably were gathered in one central place, like the big main room of the hacienda. Longarm reached the inner courtyard. An adobe staircase led up to the balcony that overlooked the

148

courtyard. He took the stairs three at a time, bounding up them while making as little noise as possible.

The room where he had spent a week recuperating from his injuries was up here. He catfooted past it, heading for the front of the house. That was where any guards were more likely to be, and he wanted to eliminate a few more of them if he could before he tried to rescue the hostages.

He froze as a door opened behind him and a man exclaimed, *"Dios!"* He started to spin around, and as he did, he saw a Mexican with a thin, hard face clawing at a holstered gun on his hip. Longarm was too far away to strike with the butt of the Winchester again. The only way to stop the man from killing him was to get off the first shot, and that would alert the entire house.

Longarm was swinging the muzzle of the rifle into line, not knowing if he was going to be in time or not, when a dark, massive shape swarmed up the balcony stairs and grabbed the gunman from behind. One huge fist closed around the man's neck, choking off any shout, while the other pinned the man's gun hand. The gunman's booted feet came up off the balcony as the hand around his neck lifted him. One sharp wrench, and with the pop of a broken neck, the man went limp.

Diablito lowered the corpse to the balcony and grinned at Longarm. "If I had the time, I would wring his head off, like the *pollo* . . . the chicken," the big *segundo* said in a harsh whisper.

Longarm heaved a sigh of relief. Diablito had doubled back to help him, just as he'd thought might have happened.

And he had brought something besides just himself. Still grinning, Diablito opened his jacket and showed Longarm the four sticks of dynamite stuck in his waistband, their fuses dangling loose. "We even the odds, no?"

Longarm motioned him closer and said, "Get to the front of the house with that stuff, then raise hell and shove a chunk under the corner."

Diablito nodded in understanding.

149

"I'm heading for the main room," Longarm went on. "I'll bet that's where the hostages are."

"*Si*, Senor Custis."

"Are you all right?" Longarm asked. Diablito's face was gaunt from the strain of being wounded.

"Do not worry about me, senor. Save your pity for those I am about to kill."

Longarm shook his head. "Not this bunch. Kill all of 'em you can, old son."

That was what he intended to do.

The American came into the main room of the hacienda and walked over to the sofa where Dulcey and Pablo sat side by side. They had been brought in here after the fighting was over and told to wait. Pablo didn't know what they were waiting for, but now as the American held out a hand toward Dulcey, he began to understand.

"Come on," the American said. "Time you and me got better acquainted."

"No!" Pablo cried out. Since his attitude toward Dulcey had changed, he had grown attached to her. He didn't want this American hurting her.

But as he started to come up off the sofa, the American put a hand on his shoulder and shoved him back down. Dulcey caught hold of him and said, "No, Pablo! It is all right. This man does not frighten me."

Pablo looked around. Three more of the gunmen were in the room, but no one else from the hacienda. The rest of Don Manuel's people were dead, Pablo knew, murdered by these invaders. He and Dulcey were the only ones left. He knew why Dulcey had been spared—the American wanted her, and no doubt the other pistoleros did, too—but why had he not been killed? He accepted his good fortune without understanding it, knowing all the while that it could end at any second, along with his life.

Dulcey got to her feet, holding herself with great dignity. "Stay here, Pablo, and do as you are told," she said. "Promise me you will do this."

"But Dulcey—" he began.

"Dulcinea," she said. "My name is Dulcinea."

"Come on," the American said impatiently. He took hold of Dulcey's arm and led her from the room.

Pablo watched them go with tears in his eyes and a lump in his throat. As they disappeared up the stairs that led to the second floor, he whispered, "Dulcinea."

Dulcey and the American had been gone for less than five minutes when the entire hacienda shook from an explosion that sounded as if the world itself were ending.

Longarm heard the blast and kicked the rear door into the main room open. He went through in a rolling dive that brought him back up on one knee. His eyes darted from side to side, taking in the scene before him. One gunman stood beside the massive fireplace, another was by the front door, and a third was beside one of the windows that looked into the outer courtyard. Smoke from the explosion boiled through that window now, and it made the gunman cough. Longarm decided to leave him for last.

From the corner of his eye, Longarm spotted the boy sitting on the sofa looking stunned. He shouted, "Pablo! Get down!" as he fired the Winchester from the hip. The slug smashed into the chest of the man by the fireplace and flung him back against the stone mantel. He bounced off and pitched face down to the floor.

The man by the door had his gun out. He fired wildly, the bullets fanging toward Longarm. Longarm levered the rifle as he brought it to his shoulder. He fired, saw the bullet turn the gunman halfway around. The man didn't go down, though. He stayed on his feet and tried to get off another shot. He and Longarm fired at the same time. The gunman's bullet burned past Longarm's shoulder, while the lawman's slug crashed through the bridge of the killer's nose and into his brain.

Longarm was swinging the rifle toward the third man when something tore the weapon out of his hands. Shock and pain jolted up his arms. He knew the gunman had fired and hit the Winchester, sending it spinning away. Longarm threw himself to the side, diving behind a heavy chair as bullets thudded into it. His hands were both numb and useless. It might be minutes before feeling returned to them, minutes he couldn't afford.

Two more shots cracked from the other side of the room, and as Longarm risked a look around the chair, he saw the remaining gunman staggering backward, his hands pressed to his chest. Blood welled between his fingers. His eyes rolled up in their sockets and he fell to the side, sprawling on the floor.

Longarm glanced back toward the fireplace and saw Pablo lying there on the floor, propped up on his elbows. The boy had a pistol in his hands. Longarm realized that Pablo had crawled over to the first man, gotten his gun, and downed the last of the three killers.

Outside, there was yelling and shooting going on, then the front door suddenly smashed open. Pablo swung the gun in that direction and almost fired before Longarm shouted, "Pablo! No!"

Pablo saw the huge figure that emerged from the thinning smoke and dropped the gun. He scrambled to his feet and cried out, "Diablito!" Then he was running across the room to throw himself into the *segundo's* bearlike embrace.

"Pablo!" Diablito said. "You are all right?"

Pablo was crying now, but he managed to nod. He threw his arms around Diablito's neck and hung on for dear life.

Longarm got to his feet and flexed his fingers. They weren't completely numb now. He was able to draw his Colt as he went over to join Diablito and Pablo.

"The others?" he asked Diablito.

"All dead," Diablito replied. He had fresh bloodstains on his left arm and right thigh, but the new wounds didn't seem to hamper him any. "They made it easy for me by standing in the courtyard together. I killed six of them with the dynamite and the others with bullets and my hands."

"What about the American? A blond man, sort of short and stocky?"

Diablito shook his shaggy head. "There were a couple of gringos, but none who looked like that. Now, after the dynamite did its work, I am afraid they look like nothing at all."

"Dulcey!" Pablo suddenly exclaimed. He turned his head to look at Longarm but still hung on to Diablito. "The American you seek, Senor Custis, he took Dulcey upstairs!"

"When?" Longarm asked.

"Just a few minutes ago."

Longarm nodded his thanks and ran for the stairs. He bounded up them, ready to settle matters at last with Peter Braddock.

But a half hour later, after an exhaustive search of the hacienda, he had to admit that the possibility he feared most had come true.

Braddock was gone—and he had taken Dulcey with him.

Chapter 14

Shortly after that, Don Manuel Escobedo and the rest of the vaqueros came galloping up to the hacienda. Longarm and Diablito greeted them at the gate. "It's over," Longarm said. "Las Hermanas del Fuego is yours again, Don Manuel."

"And the men who tried to steal it?" Escobedo asked as he dismounted.

"All dead," Diablito said.

"All but one," Longarm said.

Don Manuel looked at him, evidently recognizing the bleak tone in the lawman's voice. "The American?" he asked.

Longarm nodded. "He got away, and he took Dulcey with him."

Don Manuel paled, and his eyes widened in horror. "Dulcey?" he croaked. "Dulcey . . ."

"Don't worry, I'm going after them," Longarm said. "I scouted around but couldn't find any tracks. But I reckon Braddock will head for the border, now that his plans down here have been ruined." He frowned as a thought suddenly occurred to him. "Either that, or . . ."

"Or what, Senor Custis?" Diablito asked.

"There's some sort of connection between Braddock and Harrigan," Longarm said. "Braddock may have lit out for Harrigan's ranch." The more he thought about it, the more he realized it was a possibility he couldn't afford to overlook.

"My sister is there, too," Don Manuel said. "I must save her, must rescue her from that bastard Harrigan."

A plan was already forming in Longarm's brain. To put it into action, he would have to reveal the truth of his brief stay at Gordo Harrigan's ranch. Now that he had risked his own life to reclaim Las Hermanas del Fuego for Don Manuel, he thought it likely the man would believe his story.

"I think maybe I can get in there without Harrigan being suspicious of me," he said slowly. "That would give me a chance to get to Theresa and also to see if Braddock is there."

Escobedo frowned. "Why would Harrigan allow you to do this? I thought you were his prisoner last night."

"Well . . . sort of. You see, when I was sneaking around the place and he grabbed me, I told him that I was a hired gun who wanted to ride for him in his war against you. That seemed like the only way to play for time. It worked out later, because I was able to get away after Diablito set off his big boom."

Don Manuel stiffened and said, "You were fighting on Harrigan's side?"

"Pretending to," Longarm said. It was no use lying now. "I was in the main room of Harrigan's hacienda, using a rifle. I made sure I missed all my shots, though. When Diablito blew down the wall, I got out and came after you."

For a long moment, Don Manuel just stared at him. Then, he gave a long sigh. "I suppose I believe you," he said. "What you say makes sense, though it is an incredible story. But how will this allow us to save my sister?"

"Like I said, Harrigan believes I'm working for him. I can ride back in and claim that when you fellas lit out from his ranch, I followed you to make sure you didn't double back."

Diablito said, "And he will believe this?"

Longarm shrugged. "There won't be any reason for him not to believe it."

"But if this man Braddock has fled there, as you suspect he may have, will he not recognize you?"

Longarm scraped a thumbnail along his jawline, then grinned wryly. "Yeah, there is that little problem," he admitted. "Braddock could ruin things in a hurry. I don't need much time, though. Just a little while in the house, so I can reach Theresa, and then she and I will slip out while the rest of you stage a distraction."

"What sort of distraction?" Don Manuel asked.

Longarm's grin widened. "You know, I've been thinking about that, and here's what I've come up with . . ."

Longarm had left behind all the extra armament. He was carrying only the iron he'd had when he rode away from Harrigan's place during the night. A part of him hated to give up the Winchester, the second revolver, and the bowie. All that added killing power would have been a mite comforting as he approached Harrigan's hacienda, but he wanted to make Harrigan believe that he had followed Don Manuel to Las Hermanas del Fuego, then turned around and come straight back here.

The sun was fully up now, so he could get his first good look at Harrigan's ranch. His hastily formed conclusions the night before looked to be correct. The place was not as good as Don Manuel's, not by any means, but it wasn't terrible, either. A man could make a go of it here, with hard work and good luck, more of the former than the latter.

Of course, Harrigan was going to have to patch up the gaping hole in the front wall of the hacienda . . .

Longarm heard someone shouting as he rode up. Two vaqueros came running out of the house to point rifles at him. He tugged on the dun's mane to bring the horse to

156

a halt, then lifted both hands even with his shoulders. "Take it easy there, boys," he said. "I'm on your side, remember?"

"Parker?" a loud, angry voice said. Harrigan came limping out of the hacienda. He had a bandage wrapped around his left leg and was stripped to the waist except for bandages tightly wrapped around his torso. There was still a smear of dried blood on his forehead. "Parker, is that you? Where the hell have you been?"

Longarm inclined his head toward the ridge, on the other side of which was Don Manuel's ranch. "I followed Escobedo and what was left of his bunch," he said. "I wanted to make sure they didn't double back and attack us again."

"When I came to and nobody could find you, I got to thinking maybe the explosion blew you into little pieces." Harrigan raked fingers through his red beard. "Mighty strange the way you disappeared like that."

Longarm's face and voice both hardened. "If there's something you want to say, old son, you'd better come right out and say it. Otherwise, you might think for a minute about how I knocked you down when that dynamite came sailing our way. If I hadn't done that, you might've been hurt a lot worse."

The look Harrigan gave Longarm was equally hard, but then after a moment, he shrugged. "Yeah, I guess you're right. And you were right there fighting with the rest of us when Escobedo rode in." He gave a harsh bark of laughter. "What a stupid play that was."

Longarm didn't argue. He agreed with Harrigan that Don Manuel's attack on the ranch had been unwise. He slid down from the dun's back and led the horse to one of the corrals. He turned it in and swung the gate shut.

Harrigan said, "It's just that one of the boys says you jumped him and knocked him out as you were leaving. Why would you do that, Parker?"

Longarm swung around to face him. "Was that one of your vaqueros? Hell, the way he acted, I thought he was

157

one of Escobedo's men! All I did was defend myself."

Again, Harrigan took a few seconds to turn over that explanation in his mind, then he nodded. "Come on in the house," he said. "I reckon you could use a drink and something to eat."

"That sounds mighty fine," Longarm said.

So far he had seen no sign of Peter Braddock, and Harrigan hadn't said anything about the fugitive American. It was possible Braddock wasn't here. Longarm had known all along that returning to Harrigan's ranch was a gamble. If Braddock wasn't here, that meant he was running somewhere else—with Dulcey as his captive—and getting farther away with each passing minute.

But Longarm had been willing to take the chance. Besides, there was still Theresa Escobedo to think of, and that had tipped the scales and made him decide on this plan. As he followed Harrigan into the hacienda, he cast a glance up at the twin volcanoes looming over the countryside. From anywhere around here, the Sisters of Fire looked so close a man could reach up and touch their rocky, barren slopes.

Harrigan sat down at a rough-hewn table in the house's main room and motioned for Longarm to take one of the other chairs. He gave orders to one of the vaqueros to bring whiskey, coffee and food, then said to Longarm, "So what did Escobedo do after we chased him off?"

"Ran for home like a pup with his tail betwixt his legs," Longarm said. "He lost a sizable amount of men. He didn't look like he wanted to keep up the fight."

Harrigan nodded. "We found eight bodies. I imagine some of the men he had with him were shot up pretty bad, too."

"That's right, at least as far as I could tell. I tried not to get too close. I didn't want Escobedo to know that I was trailing them."

"Went straight back to his place, did he?"

"Yep."

Harrigan scrubbed a hand over his face. He looked very

tired. He surprised Longarm by saying, "Damn it, I wish there was some way to put a stop to all this fighting. I don't know why Escobedo's got such a burr under his saddle."

The words sounded sincere to Longarm. He said, "The fact that you kidnapped his sister might have something to do with it."

"Blast it, Theresa loves me, she's just too stubborn to admit it!" Harrigan's fist thumped against the table. "There's more to it than that, Parker. Escobedo and I were getting along fine, and then all of a sudden he starts trying to run me off my range."

Longarm knew that Harrigan believed that, and it was one of the things that puzzled him so much about this situation. Why were both Harrigan and Don Manuel convinced that the other one was out to get him? Longarm could think of only one answer that made sense.

Someone had made them believe that. But who?

The vaquero Harrigan had sent to the kitchen came back with a bottle of whiskey, a pot of coffee, cups, a bowl of beans and some tortillas. He placed the tray containing the food and drink between Longarm and Harrigan, then stepped back. Harrigan waved at the platter and told Longarm, "Dig in."

Longarm did so gladly. The coffee was especially welcome, since he had been going for so long on so little sleep. Harrigan seemed hungry, too. As the two men ate, Longarm asked in what seemed casual tones, "How'd you come to take up this place anyway, Harrigan?"

The redhead grinned across the table at him. "You mean how'd a gringo wind up running a Mex ranch? My mother was Mexican. I've lived down here along the border all my life. Fact is, nobody knows all the old smuggling trails better than I do. I rode them for a long time."

So that was it, Longarm thought—the connection between Harrigan and Peter Braddock. In his position as a U.S. Customs agent, Braddock had been taking bribes from smugglers for quite a while. That was why he was now on the run from the law. It made sense that one of the smugglers who'd been paying off Braddock could have been Harrigan.

Those thoughts flashed through Longarm's mind, but he didn't say anything, just sat there quietly as Harrigan went on, "But a fella gets tired of watching over his shoulder all the time and never being sure when somebody's going to double-cross him. I decided I wanted to get me a place and settle down. One of my cousins on the Mex side told me about this ranch. The fella who owned it had died, and his relatives down in Monterey didn't want to come run it, so I bought it from them. Fair and square, everything legal and aboveboard." He grinned. "First honest business deal I'd been in for a long time. Hell, maybe ever."

"So you just want to sit here and raise cattle and forget about those smuggling days," Longarm suggested.

"That's right. I even figured on getting married and having kids someday . . ." Harrigan looked off, his face hardening. "I thought Theresa was the woman I was going to do that with, but then everything went to hell."

The pain in the man's voice sounded genuine. Again to Longarm's surprise, he found himself almost feeling sorry for Harrigan. Harrigan had been a criminal, no doubt about it, and he was still a hard, ruthless man. But he seemed to really want to go straight, and when he spoke of Theresa, there was real affection in his voice, even now.

What if, Longarm thought, what if his guess was right and somebody *had* been playing Don Manuel and Harrigan against each other? If that was the case, then all the hard feelings between them had been manufactured by somebody else. Maybe that rift could be healed . . .

"What did Escobedo think of you, before he started trying to run you off?"

Harrigan had been guzzling coffee laced with whiskey. He lowered his cup and frowned across the table at Longarm. "What do you mean, what'd he think of me?"

160

"You said the two of you got along fine?"

"Well enough, I reckon. Shoot, you're an American, Parker. You know how the old *grandees* like Escobedo feel about gringos. He looked down on me at first, but then . . . when Theresa and I started getting closer, well, I thought her brother was warming up to me. I figured everything was going to be all right. I guess he just couldn't get over holding my blood against me."

Longarm nodded. The explanation made sense, but he still felt that something was missing. A promising friendship between the two men had been ruined. They would have been brothers-in-law if things had gone as planned.

Who stood to gain if things *didn't* go as planned?

Longarm decided it was time to up the ante. "You know a fella named Braddock? Peter Braddock?"

Harrigan looked sharply at him. "Why do you ask?"

"In my line of work," Longarm said, "you get to know a lot of folks, some of 'em no more honest than they have to be."

Harrigan let out a laugh. "And Pete Braddock was never even that honest! Yeah, I knew him, back when I was still riding the smuggling trails. Cut him in on quite a few of my deals, in fact. He works for the customs service, but he really works for himself."

"Not anymore. I heard that the law found him out, and he killed a star packer and ran."

Harrigan's bushy red eyebrows lifted in surprise. "Damn! I didn't know that. I'm not surprised, though." He leaned forward over the table. "Braddock was always a cold-blooded son of a bitch. To tell you the truth, he's one of the ones I always worried might double-cross me."

"So you haven't seen him since those days?"

"Nope. Say, you and Braddock aren't compadres, are you? Because I stand by what I said about him."

Longarm shook his head. "He's just a gent I met a time or two."

And he's also riding around on your range, giving orders to gunmen who think they're working for you, Longarm thought. If he believed what Harrigan had just told him, the information piled yet another layer of complications on top of an already tangled situation.

And yet the various pieces that Longarm had been moving around in his head were starting to come together and form more of a picture. It wasn't clear yet, but it was getting there.

In the meantime, there was still the matter of Theresa Escobedo to attend to. That plan was already in motion, and nothing Longarm could do now was going to stop it.

He ate some beans and tortillas, then said, "One thing happened this morning that was sort of bothersome. Did you hear a rumbling sound about dawn?"

Harrigan frowned again. "Come to think of it, I did. Some of the boys heard it, too. Sounded like it was a long way off."

"It was up in those mountains," Longarm said, nodding in the direction where the Sisters of Fire lay. "I looked up at them, and I thought I saw smoke coming from them."

Harrigan's eyes widened. "Oh, Lord. Really?"

Longarm nodded. "And it gave me a nervous feeling, let me tell you. I've heard that they used to be volcanoes."

"They still are," Harrigan said as he rubbed the fingertips of one hand on his forehead. "They're just dormant. Or at least they have been for a long time."

"I've heard about what happens when volcanoes blow their tops. I don't want to be anywhere around when that happens."

"As close as we are . . ." Harrigan swallowed hard. "We wouldn't have a chance."

"Well, maybe that wasn't what I heard," Longarm said, putting a blatantly false note of cheer in his voice. He knew, of course, that there hadn't been any rumblings in the mountains this morning. What Harrigan and the other men heard had been those four sticks of dynamite going off after Diablito lashed them together and tossed them in

162

the middle of the bushwhackers who had taken over the Escobedo ranch.

But Harrigan didn't know that, and Longarm's little lie about seeing smoke coming from the twin peaks just made him even more nervous.

Harrigan got up from the table and began to pace back and forth. "All the time I've been here, there hasn't been a peep from those mountains. Everybody in these parts figures they're cold, burned out inside. But I guess you never really know what's going on inside a mountain, do you?"

Longarm took out a cheroot. "I reckon not." As a matter of fact, his friend Jessica Starbuck, owner of the Circle Star ranch in Texas, had told him about being down here in northern Mexico once when a volcano that was thought to be dormant had erupted. Jessie's story had made it sound like one hell of a show. Longarm suppressed a chuckle. He was putting on such a good act for Harrigan that he was almost convincing himself.

Almost—but not quite.

He drained the rest of the coffee in his cup, then stood up, still toying with the cheroot he had taken from his pocket. "I'm mighty tired, boss," he said. "You reckon it'd be all right if I had a smoke, then turned in for a while?"

Harrigan waved a hand, not really paying that much attention to what Longarm had said. "Sure, sure, go ahead. Escobedo's whipped for now, he won't be causing any more trouble for a while."

You just go right on thinking that, old son, Longarm told himself.

He remembered from the night before where Theresa Escobedo was being held prisoner. He strolled out into the courtyard in front of the hacienda, struck a lucifer and lit the cheroot with a flourish, then turned and walked toward the outside stairs that led up to the second floor. He hoped that Diablito had been watching through the pair of field glasses, as planned, and had seen the signal.

If he had, then everything was racing toward its conclusion right now . . .

The rumbling sounded like thunder at first, a low, dull booming that steadily grew in intensity. Longarm's teeth clamped down on the cheroot when he heard it begin. He was on the stairs now. He increased his pace a little. The blasts kept coming, the sounds rolling down from the mountains that loomed over the little valley.

Longarm wasn't the only one to hear them. Vaqueros came running from the bunkhouse, the barns, and the hacienda itself. Harrigan was with them. Longarm glanced in that direction as he reached the balcony and saw that Harrigan wasn't paying any attention to him at all now. The man's frightened gaze was directed toward the Sisters of Fire, and when Longarm looked that way himself, he saw that the twin mountains were living up to their name: clouds of smoke were rolling up from Las Hermanas del Fuego.

Gordo Harrigan threw back his head and bellowed in terror, "The volcanoes—*they're erupting!*"

Chapter 15

Panic-stricken shouts filled the courtyard below as Long arm hurried along the balcony toward Theresa's room. He knew that Harrigan and the other men were convinced they were about to die. The lava that spewed from an erupting volcano was bad enough, but what was really deadly were the scalding gases that rolled down ahead of the lava, burning and blistering everything in their path. Several vaqueros screamed and ran for their horses, intending to try to outrun the deadly wave.

Longarm palmed out his Colt as he reached the door of Theresa's room. It was padlocked on this side, as he had thought. "Theresa!" he called sharply, urgently. "Theresa Escobedo! Are you in there?" He didn't want to start shooting until he was sure he had the right room, despite the evidence of the lock.

A frightened voice came back, muffled by the thick panel. "*Si*, senor. Who are you?"

"A friend," Longarm told her. "Now stand back away from the door, just in case."

He gave her a second, then blasted two shots into the lock. It jumped and shattered under the impact of the bullets, and he was able to wrench it loose. He threw a glance over his shoulder and saw that chaos still reigned around the hacienda. The rumbling sounds had stopped, but smoke still rose into the sky above the mountains. Harrigan's men ran around like chickens with their heads cut off.

But Harrigan himself had heard the shots, and he was turning around to peer up at the balcony in confusion . . .

Longarm kicked open the door of Theresa's room.

She gave a little cry and shrank back from him as he stepped into the doorway. "My name's Custis Long, ma'am," he told her quickly. "I'm a friend of your brother, and I've come to get you out of here."

The fear in Theresa's eyes dissolved into tears of relief. "At last," she gasped. "Thank God!"

From the stairs, Harrigan bellowed, "Parker!"

Still standing in the doorway, Longarm swung toward Harrigan and brought his gun up as Harrigan reached the top of the stairs. "Hold it, Harrigan!" Longarm called in a tone of command. "I don't want to shoot you, old son, but I will if I have to."

Harrigan stopped his rush, but he trembled from the violence of the emotions gripping him. "What the hell are you doing there, Parker? What is this?"

"I'm taking Senorita Escobedo away from here, Harrigan."

"Damn it, I trusted you!" Rage darkened Harrigan's face. "You'll never make it out of here alive. My men will see to that."

"I reckon that's where you're wrong. Your men are too scared right now to do anything except run away from those volcanoes."

Sure enough, most of Harrigan's vaqueros were fleeing. Quite a few of them had already jumped on their horses and were riding away down the valley as fast as they could. The ones who were left were dashing helter-skelter around the ranch headquarters, paying no attention at all to what was happening on the balcony.

"You double-crossed me," Harrigan grated. "While you

were gone this morning, you sold out to Don Manuel!"

"Speak of the devil," Longarm said, nodding toward the men who were now galloping up to the hacienda. Don Manuel and Diablito were in the lead, followed by half a dozen men. They quickly captured and disarmed the few vaqueros of Harrigan's who remained. Don Manuel looked up at the balcony and called, "Theresa!"

"Manuel!" she responded. She started running toward the stairs, anxious to get to her brother.

"Hold it!" Longarm called, but Theresa ignored him. Her path took her past Harrigan, who tensed, ready to grab her. One hand reached out toward Theresa, while the other flashed to the knife on his hip. Longarm aimed the Colt at Harrigan's head, ready to kill the man before he'd let Harrigan threaten Theresa again.

But before Longarm's finger could squeeze the trigger, Harrigan dropped his hand and stepped back, letting Theresa run past him unmolested. By the time she reached the bottom of the stairs, Don Manuel had dismounted and was waiting for her. He swept his sister into his arms and hugged her tightly, while Harrigan looked on with an expression of utter defeat on his face.

Longarm walked over to him and said quietly, "I thought for a second there I was going to have to plug you, old son."

Harrigan shook his head. "I couldn't hurt her. I've already caused her enough harm. I love her too much to do anything else. If she can't see that . . . if she won't admit even to herself how she feels about me . . . well, there's just nothing left for me to do but give up." He lifted his gaze toward the Sisters of Fire. "Anyway, it's too late now for all of us."

Longarm holstered his Colt and grinned. "Oh, I don't know about that."

Harrigan looked at him and said, "But those volcanoes—"

"Aren't doing a damned thing but sitting there," Longarm said. "What you heard was a bunch of dynamite and blasting powder going off, and that smoke came from smudge pots some of Don Manuel's vaqueros took up on the mountains as far as they could. They started early this morning, so they'd have time to get pretty high." Longarm's grin widened. "Sure looked and sounded like they were about to erupt, didn't it?"

At first Harrigan didn't believe him, but then bitter acceptance came into the former smuggler's eyes. "You planned the whole thing, didn't you? It was just a distraction so you could free Theresa and Escobedo could capture my ranch. You bastard."

"Hold on there," Longarm said, frowning now. "I wanted to turn the senorita loose, all right, but Don Manuel doesn't have any interest in taking over your ranch. He never has."

"That's a damned lie! He's been bushwhacking my men and killing my cattle and—"

"And the same things have been happening on his spread," Longarm cut in. "He blames you for that."

"What? Blast it, I never . . . I told you, I'm trying to go straight . . ."

"And I believe you," Longarm said. "It's time you and Escobedo had yourselves a good talk."

Hotly, Harrigan said, "I'm not going to talk to that son of a—"

Longarm put his hand on the butt of his gun and nodded toward the well-armed Escobedo vaqueros below. "I reckon you don't have a whole lot of choice in the matter."

Harrigan muttered some curses, but at Longarm's urging, he went down the stairs. Don Manuel and Theresa were waiting at the bottom, turning hate-filled glares on Harrigan. Longarm could see that he had his work cut out for him here. Diablito and the rest of the vaqueros looked like they were ready to fill Harrigan full of holes at the slightest excuse, and laugh while they were doing it. Longarm figured it would be best to get Harrigan and the Escobedo siblings inside somewhere.

"Let's go in the hacienda," he suggested to the three of them. "It's time you folks had a talk."

Theresa looked like she wanted to spit. "I have nothing to say to this . . . this . . ."

Don Manuel tightened his arm around her shoulders. "I am taking my sister home now," he announced.

"Not until you've heard me out," Longarm said, and his tone was hard and crisp, brooking no argument. "The three of you need to listen to what I've got to say, and there are some things you need to say to each other."

Harrigan, Don Manuel and Theresa all looked doubtful, but Longarm's tone of command was unmistakable. Of course, he couldn't really enforce it, but he was counting on them going along with him.

After a few seconds that seemed longer, Don Manuel said, "Very well. Though I swore I would never set foot in this hacienda again, I will break that vow because of the things you have done for us, Senor Custis."

"I thought your name was Parker," Harrigan said.

"It's Custis Long," Longarm said. "The sun's getting a mite hot. Let's get out of it, and I'll explain everything."

Which might prove interesting, he added to himself, because he hadn't figured out all of it just yet . . .

"My name is Custis Long," he said again after he had the three of them inside the main room of the hacienda, Harrigan in a chair by the fireplace, Don Manuel and Theresa on a sofa. Diablito stood guard in the doorway. "I don't have the bona fides to prove it right now, but I'm a deputy United States marshal."

"A lawman!" Harrigan burst out. "I should have known! A dirty, stinking law dog—"

"I'm not after you, Harrigan," Longarm broke in, "and anyway, I don't have any jurisdiction down here below the border. But I'd take it as a personal favor if you'd stop jawing for a second and listen to what I've got to say."

Harrigan folded his arms across his chest and glared at Longarm, but he was silent.

"Like I was saying," Longarm went on, "I'm a deputy marshal. I was on the trail of a fugitive named Peter Braddock when he jumped me and dropped me in the Rio Grande in Santa Elena Canyon."

"That's crazy," Harrigan said. "Nobody could survive that, especially if you went down the rapids."

Longarm grinned. "Chalk it up to dumb luck. It happened, and I lived through it. I might've died afterward, though, if a young fella named Pablo who works for Don Manuel hadn't pulled me out of the river."

"I knew there had to be some trouble involved with your circumstances," Don Manuel said. "I did not realize you were an American lawman, though."

"I didn't keep it from you on purpose. There just didn't seem to be any need to go into it while I was healing up. I sure appreciate everything you did for me, though, Don Manuel, and so does the United States Justice Department."

Harrigan said, "I understand now why you asked me about Braddock. But how'd you wind up at my ranch in the first place?"

"To answer that, let me back up to what happened yesterday morning." Longarm paused and wearily rubbed a hand over his face. Had it only been a day? It seemed a lot longer. "I was ready to head back to the border and start looking for Braddock again. Don Manuel sent a group of his vaqueros to ride with me to the Rio. Before we got there, though, we were ambushed. I was the only one who got away."

"Who bushwhacked you?" Harrigan asked.

Before Longarm could answer, Don Manuel said, "Some of your hired murderers!"

Harrigan started up out of his chair. "Damn it, that's a lie—"

Diablito swung the rifle he was carrying toward Har-

170

rigan. Longarm motioned for him to take it easy and said, "Sit down, Harrigan, and listen."

Reluctantly, Harrigan lowered himself into the chair again. "I didn't have anything to do with any bushwhacking," he muttered.

"I believe you," Longarm said.

Don Manuel looked at him in surprise. "You do?"

Longarm nodded and said, "I do. But bear with me a minute, and Harrigan, keep that Irish temper of yours under control when you hear what I've got to say." He paused, then went on, "After I got away from the bushwhackers, I managed to turn the tables on them and start trailing them. They crossed the ridge between the two valleys. At first I figured they were coming here, but they went to a camp in the foothills of the mountains, instead. While they were there, I got close enough to hear them talking, and I was there when Peter Braddock rode in and joined them."

"Braddock! I didn't know he was anywhere around here," Harrigan said.

"Well, he knows that this is your ranch, and from what he and the others were saying, it was pretty clear that bunch of gunmen thought they were working for you, Harrigan. Braddock was pretending to be the middle man between you and them."

Harrigan couldn't contain himself. He leaped to his feet and exclaimed, "That son of a bitch! I never hired any bushwhackers!"

"I figured that out for myself after awhile," Longarm said. "Harrigan, Don Manuel, both of you listen good and try to get this through your heads: all the problems you've been blaming each other for were really the work of that gang I trailed to their hideout. They *thought* they were working for Harrigan, but they really weren't."

Putting it all into words was helping Longarm get it straight in his own mind. Things were really beginning to make sense now.

"But why?" Don Manuel asked. "Why would they do such things?"

"Because somebody was trying to stir up trouble between the two of you. That ambush yesterday morning was the last straw. It caused you to ride over here with all your men, Don Manuel, and left your ranch defenseless. That was when the gang moved in and took over."

"So it was all a plan to get hold of Escobedo's ranch?" Harrigan asked, frowning as he struggled to comprehend what Longarm was saying.

"It's the best spread in all of northern Mexico," Longarm said. "I guess whoever thought up the plan figured it was worth a few months of work."

Harrigan started his usual pacing, unable to suppress the nervous energy inside him. "What you're saying makes sense," he said to Longarm, "but I don't see how Braddock figures in."

"I don't have all that figured out myself," Longarm admitted. "I don't think he was the mastermind. Until a few weeks ago, he was still working for the customs service in Eagle Pass. But there has to be some connection between him and whoever came up with the idea of taking over the Escobedo ranch. Braddock had to know that sooner or later the American authorities were going to catch on to what he was doing. He'd probably arranged things so that when he had to go on the run, he could come here and join right in on the scheme. Of course, it didn't work out and he had to take off for the tall and uncut again."

"Then all the hard feelings between Harrigan and myself," Don Manuel said slowly, "they were false?"

"I reckon the hard feelings were real enough," Longarm said. "But the reason for them was false. The two of you were manipulated into fighting each other."

Harrigan swung around sharply and faced Theresa. "Then there's no reason for you to hate me!" he said.

"You kidnapped me!" she exclaimed.

"Only because you wouldn't listen to reason! I tried to

172

tell you that I didn't do anything wrong. I tried to tell you that I love you! I couldn't stand the idea of not going through with the wedding, of not . . . of not being married to you . . ." Harrigan's voice trailed off, and his face showed clearly the misery and torment he was feeling.

Theresa stared at him, a new light in her eyes. "Gordo . . . you still . . . you still love me?"

"Of course I do!"

Harrigan took a step toward her, and Theresa started to get up from the sofa. Before they could rush to each other, however, Don Manuel said, "No! The insults cannot be forgotten. The deaths cannot go unavenged!"

Harrigan turned angrily toward him. "I didn't bush-whack your men! Weren't you listening to the marshal?"

From the doorway, Diablito said, "We left the dead bodies of our compadres here last night, murderer!"

"*You* attacked *me*, damn it!" Harrigan blazed back at him. He started toward Diablito.

Longarm got between them. "Back off, both of you!" he commanded.

On the sofa, Don Manuel let out a groan and covered his face with his hands. "Harrigan is right," he said in a muffled, miserable voice. "The blood of my men is on my hands. I acted too rashly."

Theresa tried to comfort him. She put her arm around his shoulders and said, "You did what you thought best, Manuel. It is not your fault that you were lied to."

"I let myself be fooled, and then I was ruled by my heart, not my head," Escobedo said. He lifted his head and looked at his *segundo*. "Diablito, make sure the men understand my orders. There is to be no more trouble between our vaqueros and those who ride for Senor Harrigan."

Diablito looked like he had just bitten down on some-thing that tasted bad, but he nodded. "*Si, patron.*"

"Everybody in that gang of bushwhackers is dead," Longarm pointed out. "Everybody except Braddock. And

I'm going to be getting back on his trail in a hurry now that everything's straightened out here."

"You want any help?" Harrigan offered. "I reckon I've got a score to settle with Braddock."

"As do I," Don Manuel put in. "I would have vengeance on this gringo as well."

Longarm shook his head. "I appreciate it, but I reckon it's my job to catch up with Braddock and see that he gets what's coming to him. You folks have got a lot of work to do patching things up down here."

Harrigan looked at Theresa and said, "It may take a while, but they'll get patched up, Parker—I mean, Long. You can count on that."

"Yes," Theresa agreed. "You can count on that, Senor Custis." She gave Harrigan a stern look. "Though it may take a long while indeed to make certain people see that they cannot prove their love by kidnapping other people."

"I didn't really kidnap you!" Harrigan said, waving his arms.

"I believe you did," Theresa replied haughtily.

Longarm left them talking, along with Don Manuel, and ambled over to join Diablito. The big *segundo* still wore a fierce expression on his bearded face. "I do not trust El Gordo," he rumbled.

"You'd better learn to," Longarm said with a grin. "I got a feeling he's going to be part of Don Manuel's family sooner or later."

"I fear that you are right," Diablito said gloomily. He perked up a little as he said, "You will let me ride with you in pursuit of this man Braddock, will you not, Senor Custis?"

"I wouldn't mind, but Don Manuel's going to need you around here. He depends on you."

"His mind is clearer now than it has been in a long time," Diablito pointed out. "He is himself again."

That fit right in with something that Longarm had begun to suspect. "Maybe so, but he'll have his hands full anyway."

174

"But how will you find Braddock?"

"A lot of riding and asking questions, the same way you track down any fugitive from the law. I want to go back to Las Hermanas del Fuego first, though, so I can get some sleep and a saddle and stock up on supplies before I head for the border again." Longarm grinned. "I want to say good-bye to Pablo, too."

"Braddock has Dulcey with him," Diablito said worriedly.

"I know," Longarm said. "Don't think I've forgotten about that."

After everything that had happened during this sojourn below the border, Longarm didn't think he would ever forget the woman called Dulcey . . .

Chapter 16

Longarm eased the dun to a halt in front of the cantina. Along with a tiny stone church that looked like it had been built hundreds of years earlier and a half-dozen adobe huts, the cantina was all there was to this nameless village that sat on the Texas side of the Rio Grande, northwest of Presidio. An old man with a raft had ferried Longarm across the river but had refused any payment except one of the lawman's cheroots. Longarm had said, "So long, Charon," as he rode off, and the ferryman had just grinned and bobbed his head as he chewed enthusiastically on the unlit cigar.

Now, as dusk was settling down, the strains of a mournful song played on a guitar wafted out of the open doorway of the cantina. Longarm swung down from the saddle and looped the dun's reins over the dilapidated hitch rack in front of the building. Three other horses were tied there. Longarm didn't recognize any of them.

Four days had passed since he'd left Las Hermanas del Fuego. Before that, he hadn't slept for a week as he had threatened to, but he had slept the clock around once. When he woke up, he ate a huge meal prepared by Don Manuel's cook, then inspected the dun and nodded in satisfaction at the fine saddle and the full saddlebags and the new Winchester snugged in a sheath of hand-tooled leather. Peace of a sort reigned over the area again, and Don Manuel gave Longarm credit for that.

Theresa Escobedo was back at her brother's ranch. Gordo Harrigan was going to pay court to her again, just as he had before asking for her hand in marriage the first time. Longarm was confident they would make a go of it this time.

As satisfying as it was to have put some things right, Longarm wasn't content. He couldn't be as long as Braddock was on the loose. So he had said his good-byes and ridden out. When he glanced back, he saw a massive figure and a much smaller one—Diablito and Pablo—standing side by side, still waving at him. Longarm returned the wave, then heeled the dun into a trot.

In the four days that followed, he crisscrossed the desert and the mountains, looking for tracks and stopping at every isolated *jacal* to ask the peons who lived there if they had seen Braddock and Dulcey. It had taken two days before he got his first lead, a farmer who had heard two riders pass by in the night. The next day, Longarm had found a peon who had actually seen the two people for whom he was searching. Then he had located the tracks of their horses, and he had been following them ever since.

The trail had led to this village on the Rio Grande. It was possible, even probable, that Braddock and Dulcey had stopped here. They might have replenished their supplies and ridden on.

There was a chance they might even still be here.

The old man in the corner with the guitar kept playing as Longarm walked into the cantina. His eyes stared straight ahead, milky, clouded, sightless. A quirly drooped from his thin lips, the smoke wreathing his head.

Two Mexicans sat at a table with a bottle of tequila between them, the grim determination on their faces showing just how seriously they took their drinking. A

177

young Texas cowboy stood at the bar, nursing a beer and talking nervously to the bald, bored bartender. The youngster kept casting glances toward a dark-haired woman at the end of the bar. Longarm knew the cowboy was working up the nerve to ask the woman to go out back with him. Longarm had been young himself once, about a thousand years ago, and on his good days he still remembered what it had felt like.

At times like this, though, when he was about to kill a man, he didn't feel young at all.

Peter Braddock sat at a table in the corner opposite the one where the old man played the guitar. He was pouring whiskey from a bottle into a glass. He set the bottle down, tossed back the drink, and glanced at Longarm without recognition.

Longarm hadn't shaved since leaving the Escobedo ranch. His clothes were covered with trail dust, and his face was drawn and gaunt. That probably had something to do with why Braddock didn't recognize him, but as he cast his mind back over the past two weeks, Longarm realized that Braddock had never really gotten a good look at him, at least as far as Longarm knew. Custis Long was the name of an enemy, but Braddock didn't really have a face to put with that name.

He would soon, Longarm thought.

The bartender sidled over as Longarm stepped up to the bar. "Beer," Longarm said quietly, not waiting for the man to ask him what he wanted. The bartender grunted and picked up a fly-specked mug from the shelf behind the bar. He drew the beer from a keg and set it in front of Longarm. "*Dos* bits," he said.

"Cheap at half the price," Longarm said as he slid a coin across the thick, stained planks that formed the bar.

The bartender grunted again, and for a second amusement appeared in his dark, sunken eyes. He collected the money, then went back to stand in front of the nervous, horny cowboy.

Longarm sipped the beer. It was warm and bitter, but

it cut some of the dust in his mouth and throat. He stood there for a long moment, then turned and walked toward the table where Braddock was sitting, carrying the mug in his left hand. Braddock heard the footsteps on the hard-packed dirt floor and looked up from his brooding.

"Well, son of a bitch," he said wonderingly. "You're Long, aren't you?"

"That's right, Braddock," Longarm said. "And you're under arrest." Longarm heard chairs scraping behind him and the sound of rapid footsteps as the other occupants of the cantina sensed trouble coming and lit out. The guitar fell silent.

Braddock looked at him for a second, then laughed. "Under arrest, am I?"

"That's right. Keep your hands where I can see 'em." Without taking his eyes off Braddock, he went on, "Where's Dulcey?"

Braddock didn't answer the question. Instead, he said, "You mind if I have another drink?"

"Sure, just take it slow and easy when you go to moving."

Braddock poured the drink carefully, not trying anything funny. When he had downed the liquor, he sighed and said, "Dulcey. I'd like to know where that double-crossing bitch is, too."

"Ran out on you, did she?"

"With both saddle mounts and our pack horse. Not to mention all the loot we took from Escobedo's house."

Somehow, Longarm wasn't surprised. "She planned the whole thing, didn't she?"

Braddock poured another drink without asking permission this time. "Of course she did. Some of it, anyway. Dulcey's the smartest woman I've ever known, as well as the most cold-blooded. She's a *bruja*, you know."

Longarm remembered young Pablo's talk of Dulcey being a witch. "I've never been convinced that such things really exist," he said.

"Well, they do," Braddock insisted. "There are all sorts

179

of things below the border that are too dark for gringos like us to fully understand, Long. Dulcey put a spell on Escobedo. She could make him do anything she wanted him to."

"Women been doing that to men for a long time without any magic spells."

"Oh, I'm sure the fact that she was sharing his bed had something to do with it," Braddock admitted. "But she kept his brain so muddled he looked to her to make all the important decisions."

"She probably did that by slipping him some sort of potion," Longarm said. "I've heard that the buttons from the peyote plant can make a man pretty addlepated."

"Maybe so, maybe so. I wouldn't put anything past that bitch." Braddock laughed. "Look what she did to me. Stranded me here at the ass-end of nowhere."

There were things Longarm wanted to clear up, questions he wanted answered. He started by asking, "How did you get mixed up with her, anyway?"

"Met her in Mexico City while I was down there a while back, on business for the customs service. I reckon we were what you call kindred spirits. We took to each other right away. She was about to come north to work on Escobedo's ranch. She told me about it, and I realized the spread was right next door to the place old Gordo Harrigan had taken over. I knew Harrigan, knew how hotheaded he was. I figured it wouldn't take much to stir up trouble between him and a neighbor. Dulcey agreed with me."

"So the two of you had the plan worked out before she ever came to Las Hermanas del Fuego."

Braddock shrugged. "We had the beginnings of it, anyway. I went back to Laredo and started recruiting gunmen. I sent them to Harrigan's place but told them to steer clear of the hacienda itself, and not to contact Harrigan or his men because Harrigan wanted everything kept a big secret."

"And they believed that?" Longarm asked in amazement.

"They were hired guns," Braddock said. "They weren't too smart to start with. Besides, they were getting paid. They didn't care about the details. Whenever there was a job for them, Dulcey slipped away from Escobedo's ranch and gave them their orders." He chuckled. "I think they were afraid of her, too."

"So you had all this set up to take over Escobedo's ranch—"

"And maybe Harrigan's, too, if everything worked out right."

"You figured that sooner or later you'd have to cut and run from Laredo. You wanted a place to go when that happened."

A wistful tone came into Braddock's voice as he said, "It almost worked out, didn't it? It would have if you hadn't come along, or if you had died like you were supposed to when I cut that rope and dumped you in the river." He glared at Longarm. "I'm still not sure how you lived through that. When Dulcey told me about how that kid fished somebody out of the Rio Grande below the rapids, I knew it had to be you. When she told me your name, that clenched it."

"I reckon somebody didn't want me to die just yet," Longarm said softly.

"*El Señor Dios?*" Braddock laughed. "Maybe so. But a man's luck runs out sooner or later, Long, and now yours has."

Braddock looked mighty confident, Longarm thought. He asked himself why Braddock had been so forthcoming about the details of the plan, why he had been willing to talk at length about what he and Dulcey had done. The only answer that made sense was that he was stalling for time. And the only reason he would do that, Longarm thought, was if he thought he had the odds on his side.

Dulcey hadn't run off and left him. She was still here somewhere, probably somewhere close by. And Braddock

181

was counting on her to get the drop on Longarm . . .

Suddenly, hoofbeats pounded outside and began to recede in the night. Three horses, judging by the sound. Longarm heard them plainly, and so did Braddock. The horses could have belonged to anyone.

But Braddock's eyes widened and his face paled under its tan, and he said, "That bitch. She really did it. She must've spotted you when you rode in. She really ran off."

Longarm didn't know if that was the case or not, but since Braddock believed it, he played along. "It's just you and me now, Braddock," he said quietly. "Are you coming along peaceful-like, or—"

Braddock shot up out of his chair, knocking it and the table over. The whiskey bottle and glass flew in the air. Braddock faded back, his hand clawing at the gun on his hip.

Longarm had been ready for the move. He took a step away as the table overturned, his hand already flashing across his body to the Colt in the cross-draw rig. He and Braddock cleared leather at the same instant. Braddock's gun came up just a hair faster than Longarm's, but he rushed the shot too much. His gun blasted, sending a slug whistling past Longarm's ear. Then Longarm's Colt was bucking against his palm as he triggered once, twice, then a third time.

The bullets drove into Braddock's chest and flung him back against the wall behind him. He hung there for a second as his gun slipped from nerveless fingers. The life in his eyes flickered out as blood welled from his chest. Then he pitched forward, landing in the wreckage of the overturned chair and table.

Longarm nudged the fallen gun away with the toe of his boot, then hooked it under Braddock's shoulder and rolled the man onto his back. Braddock was dead, all right, no doubt of that. With a sigh, Longarm opened the cylinder of his revolver and ejected the spent brass, then replaced the shells with fresh cartridges. He turned and looked around the room. The bartender was nowhere in sight. Probably hiding behind the bar, Longarm decided. All the customers were gone, too. Only the blind old man with the guitar still sat in the far corner, smoking.

"It's over, *viejo*," Longarm said. "I don't suppose there's an undertaker around here, is there?"

The old man's gnarled fingers thumped the body of the guitar in a peculiar rhythm. "Is a priest," he said. "He buries the dead."

"Well, there's some work for him here."

The old man grinned around the quirly in his mouth. "Is always work for one who digs graves." He laughed and plucked the strings of the guitar.

Longarm couldn't argue with that. He walked out of the cantina to see if he could pick up Dulcey's trail, and the music followed him into the night.

"Don't move now," Victoria Canfield said. The brush in her hand moved swiftly as she transferred paint from the palette in her other hand to the canvas. Abruptly, she stepped back with a frown and said, "You're moving, Custis."

"No, I'm not," Longarm said.

Victoria pointed to his shaft, which was rising into a full erection. "What do you call that?"

"Well, damn it, what do you expect? When most folks talk about nude paintings, they don't mean the artist is naked as a jaybird!"

Actually, both of them were nude as they stood in the sunlit area behind Victoria's house near Lajitas. Victoria's lean, lovely body had a few fetching splatters of paint on it. She laughed and put her brush in a cup of turpentine. "I can see we're going to have to take care of that before we can continue with the portrait," she said as she walked toward Longarm, her hips swaying slightly.

She came into his arms and he kissed her. The long, thick column of male flesh jutted between them and prodded the softness of her belly. Longarm moved his hands

183

down to the firm roundness of her rump and squeezed. Victoria worked her hips back and forth.

Longarm slid his tongue into her mouth, drinking in the hot wet sweetness of her. The hard buds of her nipples scraped against his chest. He moved his feet a little farther apart and braced his legs, then used his grip on her rump to lift her off the ground. She raised her legs and wrapped them around his hips. Longarm felt the head of his manhood teasing the slick opening between her legs. He lowered her, slowly impaling her on his shaft.

She gasped against his lips as he filled her. When he was fully inside her hotly clasping sheath, he began to thrust, slow, short, pistonlike movements that made her even wetter than before.

"Oh, God, Custis," Victoria said breathlessly, "I'm glad you came back!"

Longarm's return to Lajitas hadn't been completely voluntary on his part. He had trailed Dulcey in this direction for three days, then lost her tracks in a brief sandstorm and had been unable to find them again since then. That sandstorm had been some sort of freak of nature, he thought, blowing up out of nowhere just when he thought he was closing in on his quarry. He had spent two futile days trying to pick up the trail again, then ridden into Lajitas to replenish his supplies. As long as he was there, he thought he might pay a quick visit to Victoria.

It was turning into more than that. They had spent the night making love, then this morning she had insisted that she finish the portrait of him she had started several weeks earlier. Longarm hadn't been able to say no to her.

Victoria ground her hips against him, meeting his thrusts with her own. Longarm felt another climax building up inside him. He had already filled her with his seed several times in the past twelve hours, but Victoria couldn't seem to get enough of it. She rested her chin on his shoulder and breathed into his ear, "Give it to me, Custis. Give it to me now!"

Longarm tightened his grip on her ass, shoved his organ

184

as deep inside her as it would go, and began to spurt. He had spasmed twice when he looked past Victoria's blonde head and saw Dulcey step around the corner of the building and lunge toward them, a knife upraised in her hand.

He was too far gone to stop his climax. He kept emptying himself into Victoria. But his instincts kicked in and sent a message to his muscles that had him flinging himself sideways. Victoria cried out in a mixture of passion and surprise.

The dive took them out of the way of Dulcey's knife as it swept down, but it also sent them crashing to the ground. The impact jolted them apart. Longarm shoved Victoria one way and rolled the other way. He hit the easel and brought it down, getting tangled in its legs. He kicked it away and came to his knees barely in time to reach up and grab Dulcey's wrist as she tried to stab him.

Longarm let himself fall over backward. He heaved Dulcey with him and got a knee in her belly. She went over his head and sailed through the air. When she hit the ground, she rolled over several times, then scrambled to her feet at the same time as Longarm was getting to his. She still had the long, heavy-bladed knife in her hand.

Dulcey paused to spit curses in Spanish at him. She said, "You ruined everything!"

Longarm glanced at Victoria. She lay off to the side, shaking her head groggily. For the moment, she was out of harm's way. Longarm knew that he had to keep Dulcey distracted, though, and disarm and capture her if possible.

"I'm mighty disappointed in you, Dulcinea," he drawled. "Pablo told me you were a witch, but I never figured you for a killer and a double-crosser."

Again she cursed him in Spanish and began moving closer to him, the knife weaving seductively in the air.

Longarm ignored the curses but not the blade. "Braddock told me you ran out on him, but he was just stalling for time," Longarm said. "He was surprised as hell when you really did it."

"You killed him!" Dulcey accused.

Longarm nodded. "I sure did."

"I should kill you and your blonde *puta* for that alone!"

Longarm grinned tightly and said, "You don't give a damn about Braddock. You used him just like you used Don Manuel. You're just mad because I messed up your pretty little plan. You knew I'd come after you. You've been waiting until you could turn the tables on me and get your revenge."

Dulcey smiled. "And now I will have it. I'm going to kill you, Custis. But first I think I will cut your balls off."

They were hanging out there in plain sight, since he was naked as the day he was born. And his gun was out of reach, the belt and holster coiled on the bench next to Victoria's pots of paint. Dulcey was between Longarm and the Colt. When she came at him again, he was going to have to try to take the knife away from her before she could bury it in him . . .

Victoria was on her hands and knees now, crawling toward the fallen easel and canvas. She was behind Dulcey, where Dulcey couldn't see her. Longarm tried not to look at her for fear of warning the knife-wielding woman. Suddenly, with an incoherent cry of rage and hate, Dulcey sprang at Longarm again, sunlight flashing off the knife.

Victoria came to her feet holding the canvas and raised it above her head to slam it down on Dulcey. The canvas ripped, but the blow was strong enough to send her staggering forward. As Dulcey fell to her knees, her head poking through the large rip in the canvas, Victoria scooped up a pot of paint and brought it down. The earthenware pot shattered as it crashed against Dulcey's head. Red paint flew everywhere, drenching her head and shoulders.

Longarm kicked the knife out of Dulcey's hand and sent it spinning away. Dulcey collapsed, out cold.

Victoria stood over Dulcey's unconscious form, panting from the exertion of the fight. Some of the red paint had splashed on her, too, and as she stood there, beautiful and naked, spattered with crimson, Longarm thought she looked like some sort of warrior woman. She still held a shard from the broken pot in her hand. As she dropped it, she glared down at Dulcey and said, "That witch!"

Longarm stepped forward, pulled her into his arms, and laughed. "Darlin', you don't know the half of it!"